WITHDRAWN

THE
LAST
TREE TOWN

Also by Beth Turley

If This Were a Story

THE
LAST
TREE TOWN

Beth Turley

Simon & Schuster Books for Young Readers
New York London Toronto Sydney New Delhi

To my sister, Cristina

SIMON & SCHUSTER BFYR
An imprint of Simon & Schuster Children's Publishing Division
1230 Avenue of the Americas, New York, New York 10020

SIMON & SCHUSTER BFYR is a trademark of Simon & Schuster, Inc.
For information about special discounts for bulk purchases, please contact
Simon & Schuster Special Sales at 1-866-506-1949 or business@simonandschuster.com.
The Simon & Schuster Speakers Bureau can bring authors to your live event. For more
information or to book an event, contact the Simon & Schuster Speakers Bureau at
1-866-248-3049 or visit our website at www.simonspeakers.com.
Book design by Krista Vossen
The text for this book was set in Adobe Caslon Pro.
Manufactured in the United States of America
0320 FFG
First Edition
2 4 6 8 10 9 7 5 3 1
Library of Congress Cataloging-in-Publication Data
Names: Turley, Beth, author.
Title: The last tree town / Beth Turley.
Description: First edition. | New York City : Simon & Schuster Books for Young Readers, [2020]
| Audience: Ages 9–12. | Audience: Grades 4–6. |
Summary: Struggling with her Puerto Rican identity, her grandfather's memory loss and transfer
to a nursing home, and her sister's depression, seventh-grader Cassi joins the Mathletes at school,
finding comfort in numbers and in her new friendship with Aaron.
Identifiers: LCCN 2019028314 (print) | LCCN 2019028315 (eBook) |
ISBN 9781534420649 (hardback) | ISBN 9781534420663 (eBook)
Subjects: CYAC: Sisters—Fiction. | Depression, Mental—Fiction. | Mathematics—Fiction. |
Friendship—Fiction. | Puerto Ricans—United States—Fiction.
Classification: LCC PZ7.1.T875 Las 2020 (print) | LCC PZ7.1.T875 (eBook) | DDC
[Fic]—dc23
LC record available at https://lccn.loc.gov/2019028314
LC eBook record available at https://lccn.loc.gov/2019028315

Summer

1

The Way Hearts Do

On the first day of seventh grade, I calculate the distance between my sister and me. We're five miles apart. If it were last year, Daniella would be somewhere in this building, taking notes on Joan of Arc in history class or picking cheese off cafeteria pizza. Now a great gust of wind has swept her 26,400 feet away, to Mapleton High School.

I dial the combination for my new locker. 13-27-31.

It's been thirty-one days since I sat cross-legged on my bed while Daniella painted my nails sparkly blue. (Twenty-seven days of August, plus four days in July.) This can't be what teachers mean when they say we'll use math in real life. Adding the number of days since you last heard your sister's laugh. I stuff my binders into the locker and shut the door.

"Gah," I blurt. Mr. Garrison, my sixth-grade algebra teacher, is standing in front of me with a wide grin and a fluorescent pink piece of paper in his hand. His tie has division symbols on it.

"Congratulations, Cassi," he says as if I've done

something extraordinary. As if I didn't just make a noise in his face like one of those screaming goats.

"For what?" I try to catch my breath.

"Your grades from last year qualify you for Math Olympics." He hands me the piece of paper. "What do you think?"

I would dance up and down the hall if I could. But I have about as much rhythm as a raisin.

"I'll be there," I say, instead of the dancing. A smile stretches so wide across my face that I can almost see my cheeks. Mom says Daniella and I have the same smile, sister smiles, but I think that's because we have the same bottom teeth. Crooked, but not quite enough for braces.

Mr. G high-fives me. Almost all the blue polish on my nails has chipped off, but one tiny speck still clings to my thumb like it can't let go. I use an old piece of tape to hang the flyer in my locker. Things look brighter now. For the rest of the day, I trace the word "Math" on the flyer every time I take out a binder.

I find Mom in the kitchen after school. Mondays are her day off from working at the Mapleton Library.

"Mom, guess what?" I take the chair next to hers. Her fingers wind up in her black hair the way they do when she's stressed. The last time I saw her sitting like that was when the town council wanted to cut the library's budget in half. Mom fought back, going to all the town meetings and typing emails on her laptop late at night until the council changed its mind.

A newspaper sits on the table, opened up to the puzzle page.

The smell of burnt coffee in the kitchen + mistakes on Mom's sudoku (difficulty level: two out of five stars) = Nothing good.

"Tell me, *mi amor*," she says. Mom writes the number six in a box, looking too tired to fight against town councils or anything else.

"It can wait. . . ." I let my voice fade away. I fold over the edge of the place mat, a laminated parrot. "There's already a six in that row."

Mom sits in front of the blue jay place mat. We have a whole set of bird place mats, each one shaped as a different kind of bird. It's like our kitchen table is a bird sanctuary. She studies the puzzle and then smiles at me in a watery way.

"Will you try to talk to your sister? I told your dad to bring home her favorite pizza for dinner."

My stomach dips.

"She won't listen to me," I tell her. *She's ignored me for thirty-one days.*

"Please." Mom doesn't say it like I have a choice. I shove the chair back. The movement shifts the parrot-shaped place mat, so that it looks like it fell onto its face.

Daniella's room is across from mine. Three feet apart. A sign on the door spells out her name in tiny, turquoise seashells. We collected the shells with Buelo and Buela in Mayagüez, the town in Puerto Rico where they lived until Mom turned thirteen. I have a name sign like Daniella's too. "Cassandra" is spelled out in pebbles. No one calls me that, except this sign, and my cousin Jac when she wants to be dramatic. Which is often.

I knock once, twice, three times. A shell is missing from one of the *L*s. I knock again. When she doesn't answer, I open the door. Daniella's doorknob has a malfunction. It was installed the wrong way, so it only locks from the outside. Dad is always telling Daniella he'll fix it. I secretly like that she can never lock herself away from me. Not completely at least.

Her desk is straight ahead, facing the window. Daniella sits looking at the sunset. She is bronze shoulders, yellow tank top straps, dark curls hanging over the chair. A sister in pieces.

My heart hollows out the way hearts do when they see something so sad that it's almost unbearable.

"Dinner soon," I tell her.

"Okay."

Her backpack spills out on the throw rug by her bed. I see a navy pencil case, a wooden ruler, a textbook. The spine says *The Chemical Property of Life*. It seems like the kind of book that would answer big, important questions. Like how my sister could swipe blue polish across my nails one night, and be somebody else the next morning.

I want to ask Daniella everything about her first day of high school, like if she got placed in American Studies and had the same lunch period as her friend Jenna. She told me she was worried about that.

"I've been told there will be Pepper's Pizza. Extra crispy, extra pepperoni, light cheese."

"O-*kay*."

The word cuts sharp, like stepping on a broken shell. I stop myself from thinking that Daniella is a broken shell. Because she's *not*. Because she can't be. My hand hovers above the doorknob. I guess it doesn't matter whether something locks from the inside or outside. No one can get in either way.

2

Pepper's Pizza

My family sits at the table that night at our bird place mats. The pizza box is open between us. Pepper's Pizza puts a single red chili pepper in the center of all their pizzas. Daniella used to pick it off and wave it in front of my face.

"Five dollars if you eat this," she said.

"Three days of math homework if you eat it," my sixth-grade self answered.

"No TV if you keep playing with your food," Mom chimed in. Dad nodded like he agreed but half smiled while doing it.

Daniella and I paused for a second, laughter trapped in our throats, and then she stuck the pepper into her mouth. She looked at me, victorious, while she chewed. Her dark brown eyes began to water from the spice.

"Geometry for you," she teased.

Tonight the pepper sits on the pizza, curved like a skinny, red smile.

"Big day, *mi amor*," Mom says to Daniella. "High school. Did you like your teachers?"

"Sure," Daniella answers. Her hand balls into a fist

on the toucan place mat. Her eyes are fixed on its long, orange beak, like she wants it to say something. When we first got the bird place mats, Daniella claimed the toucan because she was obsessed with Froot Loops cereal.

"Did you find your way around okay?" Dad adds.

"Yes."

I stare so hard at the pepperoni slices that they turn to deep, dark holes. I want to disappear inside one and end up in a world where Daniella still dares me to eat spicy peppers.

"So a good day, then?" Mom pulls another piece of pizza out of the box and puts it on Daniella's plate, even though she hasn't finished her first one. Mom's movement makes the red pepper flip over. It's frowning now.

"It was *fine*."

Dad flinches. Mom opens her mouth and closes it again. I reach quickly for the pepper and scarf it down. It tastes like fire. Daniella looks at me for a second before turning back to the toucan. It doesn't look anything like the one on a Froot Loops box.

The kitchen is quiet with the sound of no one knowing what to say. I take a bite of my pizza and pretend the tears on my face are from the spice.

3

Sunburn

My cousin Jac dyed her hair blue with Kool-Aid. She said she read about doing it in an article online, and that it was supposed to wash out in five days. It's been three weeks. I sit outside the cafeteria at a picnic table with her and our friend Ben Chay. We get twenty minutes of free time after lunch. The late August heat presses down on me. I take off my cardigan.

"You even burn through sweaters," Jac says, and pokes my shoulder, where a red blotch blooms across my ivory skin.

"So do you," I remind her.

"Yeah, but you're the one with Puerto Rican genes." Jac is my cousin on my dad's side, which is where I get my copper-colored hair and skin that burns easily in the sun. Buela calls me "*Fantasma*," which means "Ghost." *Take care of this skin,* Fantasma, she reprimanded during our trip to Puerto Rico when I was nine, while she slathered my arms in SPF 70. Her accent wrapped around the word and made it sound pretty.

From my spot in the shade, I noticed for the first time

how Daniella's skin glowed when she lay on her striped towel. Like she was made of gold and Mayagüez sunshine. I was made of freckled white sand and SPF 70.

"Tell us about Math Olympics," Ben says. He shimmies to the song pouring out of his headphones, eyes bright brown, his dark hair cut neat around his ears. His T-shirt says *Caution: May Spontaneously Burst into Song* in letters that look like spray paint. A very accurate warning.

"It's boring," I lie.

"If it matters to you, it's not boring." Jac smiles. The corners of her mouth curve into her cheeks like carvings. I shiver, which is exactly what she wants. She knows her smile is spooky, and she embraces it wholeheartedly. I think about Jac and Ben and Daniella and me sitting outside by the fire pit Dad built in our backyard. The last time we were out there, Jac held a flashlight under her face and grinned.

"You're supposed to say something, Jac. Not make faces. Tell us a story," Daniella said with a mouth full of s'more. The air smelled like smoke and summer.

"Are you not still scared?" she asked, letting her smile sink deeper.

"I am not." Daniella laughed while Ben and I quietly compared our goose bumps.

We called ourselves the Chordays, a combination of Ben's last name and ours, like we were our own family. Like a day of the week that no one knew about but us.

I shove away the thought.

"Okay. Well, you can't join until seventh grade, and we get together every week to work on different kinds of problems that might show up on the monthly evaluations, which are like mini practice competitions, and after we take those, our correct answers get added together as a group, and then that number gets sent to the Math Olympics committee, and if we get enough correct answers, then we can qualify for Regionals and States and even Nationals."

It comes out in one big breath, everything I didn't get to say at dinner last night. When I'm done, I feel like I've been underwater for a while.

"You're right. That is boring." Jac smiles again. The sun hides behind a cloud.

"Jac! Don't be mean to our genius," Ben says.

"Cassandra knows I'm kidding. If I'm mean to the genius, who'll do my algebra homework?"

"Maybe . . . you?" he replies.

I laugh. Sometimes I wonder if Jac and Ben would be friends if they didn't grow up in the Lakeside Townhouses together. Or if Jac and I would be friends if we didn't share an age and a last name. Or if Daniella only hung out with us because she felt like she had to. But maybe it doesn't matter how we all became friends or if we should've been. It only matters that we were. *Are.*

"Come over after school," Ben says to me. "Mom made kimchi for Dad's birthday. It's *fully* fermented."

My mouth waters at the thought of Mrs. Chay's kimchi, spicy and sour at the same time. She makes big Tupperware containers of it for special occasions, like birthdays and Daniella's eighth-grade graduation.

"I can't. We're visiting Buelo," I answer. "But tell Papa Chay happy birthday."

"Is Dani going with you?" Jac's eyes drop to the picnic table, like she might find Daniella there.

"Of course. Why wouldn't she?"

The question falls, as heavy as a rock, between us.

Jac pokes my sunburn again. Ben fidgets with his headphones. I do a quick calculation. It's been forty-seven days since our last night of s'mores and scary stories. The number forty-seven has too many sharp edges.

"Are you going to forget us when you go to high school?" Ben asked in the voice he uses during school plays, strong enough for the back row to hear him.

"Hey." Daniella held up her hand. "You all can't get rid of me that easy."

The bell rings to signal the end of free time. All us seventh graders shuffle like a herd of sheep back into Eliza T. Dakota Middle School. I want to stop thinking about the way Daniella looked at dinner, so different from that night around the fire. Like every part of her face was working hard not to crumble.

I focus on the back of Jac's head. Her hair matches the sky.

4

Kindly Vines

Kindly Vines Nursing Home smells like reheated vegetable soup and bleach. Breathing the air in makes my stomach hurt a little. I walk with Mom and Daniella down the maze of halls to Buelo's room, number 201, across from a sitting area with uncomfortable chairs. Sometimes we pick Buela up from her condo on Smith Street before we come, and sometimes she drives herself in her little gold car. She has to sit on two pillows to see out the front window.

A few women from Saint Anthony's are in Buelo's room already. They wear polyester pantsuits and gush over Daniella and me. One of them, Ms. Sonia, taught the Communion class I took at the church in fourth grade. Buela walked me in on the first day.

"This is Fantasma," *she said. I started to write* "Fantasma" *on the sign-in sheet but crossed it out and wrote "Cassi."*

I sat down in a circle with some of the girls in my class. They whispered in Spanish that my hair looked like the inside of a scarecrow's arm. When Ms. Sonia had us go around the room introducing ourselves, I said, "Soy Cassi y yo hablo español." I'm Cassi and I speak Spanish. The girls shifted in their seats. Maybe my hair sort of looked like scarecrow stuffing shooting out in frizzy directions, but I'd never thought too much about it until I'd heard their whispers.

That night I rubbed globs of Daniella's gel into my dry hair to smooth down the sticking-out parts. But I just ended up with stiff tangles.

The women side-kiss my cheeks, speaking with rich, tilted accents. "*Que linda.* So pretty and grown-up."

"*Gracias,*" I say. I may speak Spanish, but I can never make it sound natural. Not like Mom or Buela or the women from Saint Anthony's.

"I am a lucky man." Buelo's raspy voice comes from behind the wall of church women. I politely step around them. Buelo looks small, and his tan skin is papery. I'm careful when I hug him, because sometimes I worry his bones will break if I squeeze too hard.

"Hi, Buelo," I say.

"My *corazónita.* Daniella," he whispers into my ear.

"That's Cassi, Pico," Buela reminds him from the rocking chair next to his bed.

I try not to let his slipup hurt. I'm his *corazónita* too, and he still remembers that part. I step away from Buelo's bed so the real Daniella can hug him. Buela takes my hand. I can smell her powdery perfume. She has short silver hair and the world's softest skin.

"Thank you for coming," she says. A blue paper-weight holds a balloon down on the table behind her. The balloon says *Keep Your Chin Up*.

"I come all the time," I say.

"*Sí*, but you don't have to. You could grow right up and forget your grandparents."

The way Buelo is forgetting me.

"Never, Buela."

I want to smile or laugh, but it's hard with the sharp, soupy smell and Buelo's wheelchair in the corner. It reminds me that we might not collect seashells or pebbles again. That he might never tell another story. Buelo has lots of stories, but the one he told us the most was from his first day of school, when his teacher decided his name wasn't real. Buelo tried to explain to his teacher that "Pico" *was* a real name, because it was *his* name, but she didn't listen. She said from that point on he would be Eduardo, and he was. His high school diploma even says "Eduardo."

"*That can't be true,*" *Daniella said when he first told us the Eduardo Story, and I nodded in agreement.*

"*I mean it,* corazónitas." *Buelo's smile touched his glasses.*

Sometimes I want to ask Buelo to tell the Eduardo Story, but I'm too scared he won't remember it.

"Why don't you step outside for a second, Cassi," Mom says. She puts a hand on Buela's shoulder. "It's crowded in here."

Kindly Vines

The church women call me *linda* again on my way out. I don't see Daniella in the room anymore. I pause outside the door for a second, and the hushed voices start behind me.

Kicking me out of the room + quiet talking = Things are bad with Buelo.

I step into the bathroom that's a few feet away from Buelo's room. Daniella is there at the sinks in a black dress. She turns to me, her face blank, my sister but not quite. Like a smudged pencil drawing of herself. I walk to the sinks.

"It must be weird for you," she says.

"What do you mean?" Nerves gather in my stomach.

"To be around all these Spanish people when you don't look Spanish at all."

I glance at her reflection.

"But I am." I force a laugh. "I'm the same as you."

"Just saying." Daniella shrugs.

"Buela is teaching me to roll my *R*s better. And it's not my fault I'm sensitive to the sun." I press my hand to a red, burnt spot on my arm, trying to cover it up.

"This isn't about the sun, Cassi. It's always like this. You're always like *that*."

She says "that" the way someone would say "wrong" or "bad" or "lost." I watch Daniella tug her dark curls, adjust her dress, and walk out. My heart prickles the way it did when the girls in my Communion class thought

I couldn't speak Spanish. Like it did at the Welcome to Middle School dance for sixth graders last year, my first school dance ever.

Ben, Jac, and I were in a spot at the edge of the dancing area. All the popular kids were in the middle. Part of me wanted to be there in there with them, where the chaperones kept breaking up couples that were dancing too close, but I wouldn't have known what to do if I had been in the center. My body moved too awkwardly to the music, like my limbs and the song couldn't communicate with each other. I imagined a spotlight beaming down on me, showing the whole world I wasn't ready for a Welcome to Middle School dance. I told Jac and Ben I'd be right back and went to stand by the refreshment table. I watched my best friends—one whose whole life was a musical number and the other who didn't know how to care what people thought. I stayed in my spot in the corner and drank fruit punch until the sugar made me queasy.

Daniella had her door open when I got home.

"Hey, I've been waiting for you. I want to hear everything," she called out.

I didn't answer. I closed the door hard and curled up in my bed. The pebble CASSANDRA *sign banged around. I knew how the sign felt. Rattled.*

Daniella came in a minute later. I didn't have to look to be sure it was her. I knew the sound of my sister's footsteps. She sat on the edge of my bed.

"What happened?" she asked.

"I don't fit in," I answered.

"Fitting in is overrated."

"Of course you can say that. You always fit in. Every-where."

Daniella put a hand on my shoulder and tried to roll me over. I wouldn't budge.

"Want to tell me what we're talking about here?"

I tried to stop thinking about dancing with boys, and big bowls of blood-red fruit punch. About women on TV who dance in bright dresses with flowers in their hair. About my own family who flew in from Florida and Puerto Rico for my grandparents' fiftieth anniversary party, the Spanish music loud, their movements as smooth as water.

"I can't dance. I'm supposed to be able to dance. Like you and Mom and all the Titis."

Daniella laughed under her breath.

"It's meant to be fun, Cass. If you only focus on how you look, then it's not going to be," she said, and then stuck her arms under my body and tried to lift me.

"What are you doing?" I shouted.

"Either come on your own or I will carry you."

I didn't move. Daniella picked me up. I pretended to struggle as she brought me across the hall to her room and then deposited me onto her carpet.

"Now what?" I asked.

Daniella set up her speaker, and it started playing a fast song with lyrics in both Spanish and English.

"Dance," she said.

I crossed my arms.

"Did you not hear me before? I can't."

She reached out and grabbed my hands. Her hips swung to the music, her arms moving to the same beat of the song, taking mine along.

"Yes. You can. Just move." She mouthed the lyrics.

I started with my feet, little side to side movements that I tried to match to Daniella's. Then my shoulders joined in with circle motions.

"Like this?" I asked.

"However you want! That's the point." Daniella smiled our same sister smile. The song's chorus started again, and I let myself move until I was too dizzy and breathless to care what I looked like.

I guess it's not good enough to stumble around on Daniella's carpet anymore. I need mathematical proof of who I am—a tan color in my skin or a dark, satiny shine to my hair. Hips that know what to do when a song comes on. But in the mirror there is only paleness and red patches. Long, rhythm-less arms. Split ends like dried-out straw.

I walk out of the bathroom. Either the hallway has changed or I have. Everything is upside down. Buela steps out of the room.

"Come, *Fantasma*. We're doing a prayer."

Ghost. The word punches and leaves a bruise. She

doesn't call me *"Fantasma"* because I'm special. She does it because I'm different.

I walk back into room 201 and stand next to Mom. I bow my head while the church women recite the Hail Mary in Spanish. My legs stick out from my shorts, strikingly white, and tears burn hot in my eyes. I'm afraid to look away from my knees, or at Daniella, or at the women with their rosary beads. If anyone *really* looks at me, they'll see what Daniella sees. They'll realize I'm not one of them.

I'm in a classroom I've never seen before. The floor is made of sand instead of tile. Seashells are scattered all over. I reach down for a fan-shaped one close to my feet, but it moves farther away each time I try to grab it.

"Cassi Chord," I hear a voice say. I straighten back up. A teacher stands in front of the classroom with an attendance sheet.

"Here," I answer. The teacher's eyes scan across the sand. "Cassi Chord?"

There's no one else in the room.

"Here," I say louder.

The teacher looks back and forth again. A chart on the wall features perfectly round, colored circles, the names written underneath in Spanish. Café, verde, azul. *Colors of the earth and trees and water.*

"I'll say it one more time. Cassi Chord."

19

The Last Tree Town

My heart fills with anger and fear and loneliness.
"I'm Cassi," I scream. "I'm Cassi!"
The teacher finally looks at me over her thin, wiry glasses.
"No. You're not."

5

Mapleton

Math Olympics meets in Mr. G's classroom. The windows face the parking lot, and the digits of pi border the walls on glossy strips of paper. Mr. G had us memorize the first thirty numerals as part of his algebra class last year. Sometimes I wonder how a brain decides what to hold on to. Like, I've forgotten who was at my sixth birthday party, but I can remember that my name was spelled wrong on the cake. *Happy Birthday, Cassy.* Daniella tried to fix it, but the letters smeared together.

I sit at a desk by the window and don't let myself think about the nightmare. *There is no sand and no shells. This is where you learned about prime numbers.*

"You should all be proud of yourselves." Mr. G stands in front of the lesson he's written on the board. *Lesson One of Math Olympics: Begin with the process of elimination. What doesn't belong?* His tie is covered in sevens. "You needed an A average in your math courses to get here, and you've done it."

I look around to see who else is in the room. Sage Gordon is in the front row, wearing a blue sundress with yellow flowers. Her hair is white-blond, like Jac's before she put Kool-Aid in it. Everyone calls her "Sage the Great." At the Welcome to Middle School dance, she had her hair in spiral curls, and danced with three different boys. I remember thinking that she'd never be stuck in a corner with a fruit punch mustache. I guess that's one of those things my brain decided to hold on to.

Sage's best friend, Allie Prince, sits behind her. The boy to Allie's left must be new because I've never seen him at school before. Emilio Rivera is in the seat next to me. His skin is tan and shiny. He was in my Communion class at Saint Anthony's. I wonder if he heard those girls talk about my scarecrow hair. I run a hand across my head to tame the fly-aways.

"Does anyone have any questions?" No one raises a hand. Mr. G shrugs. "I guess I have nothing to teach you, then. Club dismissed."

"What are the competitions like?" Allie blurts. Her hair is pulled up in a perfect red ponytail. Her lacy white shirt shows the freckles on her arms.

"The one question I can't answer. I've never had a club qualify, seventh or eighth grade. Are you all going to be my first?"

We cheer back at him. I'm all wrapped up in numbers the way Mr. G's classroom is wrapped in pi.

"You'll have to become a team. That means getting to know each other better. Starting with . . ." He drops his voice low. "Two truths and a lie. Pick a partner and break that ice." He imitates breaking something. It looks like he's pulling a heart apart.

Sage picks Allie. Emilio pairs with Markus Ferris, who wears his hair in cornrows and takes a pre-calculus class at the high school. I feel a pang of appreciation for Jac. She always claims me as her partner during group work. In Metals last year, she hissed like a cobra if anyone else tried to be my Drill Bud (Mr. Windsor's take on "drill bit").

"You can pair with Cassi-no-*e* Chord," Mr. G says to the new kid, like the most remarkable thing about me is that my name is missing a letter.

Insanely tall (almost two yardsticks) + beige T-shirt and olive-green cargo shorts + shaggy brown hair falling into his eyes = The new kid.

"Should I go first?" he asks when he sits at the desk in front of mine. His voice sounds like it comes from deep in his chest.

"Sure," I say.

He sits up straighter.

"This is the fifth town I've lived in with a tree in its name. I build incredible birdhouses. I'm actually terrible at math."

I search for clues. The new kid has rough patches on his hands, which could confirm the birdhouse thing. The living in five towns might be a lie. Or maybe it seems far-fetched to me because I've lived in Mapleton my whole life.

"Any guesses?" the new kid asks.

I clear my throat and my thoughts.

"Your lie is that you're bad at math. You wouldn't be here if you were."

"Correct. Ten points to Cassi-no-*e* Chord," he says.

"Just 'Cassi' is fine," I say.

"I'm Aaron Kale." He pushes his hair out of his face. I look closer at this birdhouse builder who has lived in five towns named after trees. His eyes are amber-colored. He has three birthmarks plotted like an acute triangle on his neck. It's a funny list of things to know about someone.

Maybe that's just how people get to know each other. In little sets of facts.

"Why have you moved so much?" I ask. Aaron shifts in his seat like I threw a heavy weight on him.

"My dad is writing a memoir about a father-son trip through tree towns. But to write a memoir you have to live the memories first. So that's what we're doing."

I imagine myself as a pale birch tree, my branches stretching upward to a sleet-gray winter sky. I think Aaron would be an oak. He seems pretty sturdy.

"What were the other tree towns like?"

He shakes his head.

"You can't get out of this that easy. It's your turn. Lie to me."

In my head, Daniella's voice says, *You can't get rid of me that easy.* I see her face lit by the fire pit, feel the air like a warm cloud around the Chordays.

I push her lie away and come up with my own.

"I'm Puerto Rican. I've broken a bone. And I have a cousin who also goes to this school."

"You're not Puerto Rican."

He says it so fast. His words are like thorns pressed into my ghost-white bark—I mean, skin.

"Why'd you guess that?"

Aaron points to *Lesson One of Math Olympics.* "I eliminated."

"Show your work," I say, like a teacher writing on a test in red pen. Aaron's forehead creases.

"Well, I met a Jac Chord in my English class earlier, so I'm assuming that's your cousin. Nice hair, by the way. And you don't really look Puerto Rican, but you do look strong enough to handle a broken bone."

"And how does someone *look* Puerto Rican?" Anger laces my question, ignites in my chest. I add *too quick to assume* to my set of Aaron Facts.

"Uh. I picked the wrong one. I'm really sorry." He waits for me to say something. I don't. "I'll quit Math Olympics right now if you want me to. Seriously."

Aaron grips his chair, ready to push himself up. I think he might actually walk out if I tell him to. He reminds me a little of Jac.

Mr. G taps a marker against the whiteboard. The class quiets down.

"Watch your step, people, because you broke the ice all over this place." He pretends to wobble on slippery ground.

Aaron doesn't go back to where he started. He keeps facing me.

"I'll make you a deal," he says. "Forgive me, and I'll tell you a story from every tree town I've lived in."

Stories like Buelo used to tell + befriending a stranger = Maybe forgetting to feel like a stranger in my own skin.

But the anger still feels too hot for me to forgive him just yet.

"I'll think about it," I say. He nods and turns around.

Mr. G starts his lesson on the process of elimination. It can be used on all types of problems, like multiple choice or true-or-false. He tells us that sometimes a problem will trick us with unnecessary information. We can eliminate that, too.

Sunlight glares off the late buses outside an hour later. Mr. G dismisses us, and I see Mom's maroon minivan parked in the lot, waiting for me. A folded piece of paper slides across my desk while I pack up my notes and new Math Olympics workbook.

"The first story. I hope it helps with your decision," Aaron says. He slings his backpack over his shoulder before walking out. I unfold the piece of paper.

Mapleton: I met Cassi Chord, cousin of Jac Chord. She is Puerto Rican. She has never broken a bone.

A set of Cassi Facts.

6

Shavasana

Six.

Mom squeezes Daniella's leg and whispers "*Todo estara bien*" for the sixth time since we left for Saturday Yoga in Carnation Park. *Everything will be fine.* Mom saw the ad for yoga in the Mapleton Parks and Rec catalog. She circled it with the pencil she uses for sudoku and stuck it to the fridge with a magnet from Pepper's Pizza.

"I don't really feel like going," Daniella said before we got into the car this morning.

"That's exactly why we are doing it. A few deep breaths of fresh air can change a person's entire mind-set." Mom blocked the front door like she wasn't letting Daniella back inside, no matter what she said.

I think it would take an oxygen tank of fresh air to change Daniella's mind-set.

"Aunt Flora, is it true there's a yoga pose where you lie there and do nothing?" Jac asks from the bucket seat next to mine. She has her hair tied up in two blue buns.

"You don't do nothing. You breathe. You reflect," Mom says.

"But the 'lying there' part is true," Jac says.

Daniella whips her head around. "Do you ever turn off?" she snaps.

I expect Jac to flash her creepy smile and say, *Never.* Instead her eyes widen and shift to the window. Daniella's always been the one to call Jac out on her antics, but not like *that.*

"Be nice," Mom whispers.

Daniella leans her head to the side. Her dark braid swings. The Carnation Park sign is ahead, obscured by flowers and ferns and grass. We drive through the entrance and into the dirt lot.

"Sorry," Daniella mumbles, like she's apologizing to her reflection in the window.

"Todo estara bien." Mom squeezes Daniella's leg again. I wonder if she's saying it more to herself than Daniella.

Seven.

We park, and Jac bursts from the minivan. Mom gets out too. For a second it's just me and the back of Daniella's head. I wonder if she'd even turn around if I screamed.

Mom hands me a purple yoga mat from the back when I get out. Jac has the blue one tucked under her arm. Mom takes out the two pink ones left and closes the door. She leans them up against the car, then looks at us.

"Your cousin doesn't mean to take her feelings out on you, Jac. She's going through some growing pains."

"What are those?" Jac asks.

Mom smiles tightly. "It's like how your knees hurt when you get taller. Except it's her heart stretching out in difficult places. The pain goes away in time."

Jac nods and waves her yoga mat around like an oversize magic wand. Like she can conjure up a spell to take Daniella's growing pains away. Mom taps on the back window. Daniella doesn't move.

"Go ahead. We'll meet you." She hits the glass with her whole palm this time.

Jac and I walk toward the open field. A few women are out there, unrolling their mats in the sun-scorched grass. Some of their leggings are black, some are leopard print, and some are bright neon like Easter eggs.

"How long do you think those growing pains last?" Jac asks, tugging on one of her buns.

I look over my shoulder. Daniella still hasn't gotten out of the car. I try not to think of her heart being stretched like a rubber band.

"Until it stops hurting, I guess." Our flip-flops slap the concrete.

"We were all supposed to stick together even when she went to high school."

"We are. Like super-est superglue." I don't even convince myself. The two-year difference between Daniella and the rest of us never mattered before. Now we might as well be a hundred years apart.

"'Super-est.' Interesting. Maybe stick to the math."

The field is wide and turns into woods at the edges. A wooden fence separates the field from the parking lot. I walk through the gap in the beams. Jac leaps over them.

We lay our mats in the back row, leaving room for Daniella and Mom. Daniella sets her spot up next to mine but puts five feet of space between us. Farther than the distance between our bedrooms.

The yoga instructor's name is Lola. She wears striped leggings and a matching headband.

"Welcome," she says. I can tell she's trying hard to sound serene. "This class is designed for all skill levels. Follow along with what you can. I'll come around and show you how to modify what you can't."

Lola folds into different positions. The class copies her moves. I lunge and bend and lift my arms, face leaned up to the sun, lungs full of fresh air. Lola calls it the Warrior pose. Maybe Mom was right about the transformative power of a deep breath. It does adjust my mind-set.

The "lie down and do nothing" pose is called Shavasana.

"Roll gently to a lying position. Do not under-emphasize this pose. It is critical to your practice," Lola says. She demonstrates Shavasana.

"Finally." Jac lies down, arms and legs spread into a yoga-mat angel.

I turn toward Daniella. She rests on her back with her eyes closed and arms pressed tight to her sides. A tear wedges in the corner of her eye. It gleams like a diamond. I look away.

I'm still mad at her for the way she made me feel at Kindly Vines, and the way she's shut the Chordays out. So mad and confused sometimes that I think I'll self-destruct.

But that doesn't mean I want to see her cry.

7

Humpty Dumpty

I wake up the next day with the sun in my eyes and a plan to sneak into Daniella's room when she's not there. I've never gone behind her back like that before, but that's because I've never had to. Daniella used to keep her door cracked open. I could peek inside and find her propped against her pillows, listening to music.

"Come in already," she said when she saw me. Her bed had twelve decorative throw pillows. Each one was different. I leaned into the square one covered in sequins and watched our reflections in her mirror, which had handwritten notes and Polaroid pictures taped to it, while a slow song played out of her speakers. I listened closely to the lyrics. The singers were always losing the person they loved most.

"Why do you like sad songs?" I asked her.

"They make you feel things," she answered, and sunk deeper into her striped body pillow. "They make you feel understood."

Those moments were different from the time when we danced on her carpet. We were quiet and still while the music put words to the feelings that we couldn't.

Now her door is always closed.

A car pulls into our driveway. I peek through my blinds and see Jenna's mom's Jeep. Daniella comes out of the house.

"Going to the mall. Be back later," she calls out behind her. Everything is muffled—Daniella's voice, the front door closing, the Jeep driving off. The way sounds get when you watch something from far away. I roll out of bed and pull on my holiday fuzzy socks. They're the quietest on our hardwood floors.

My shadow darkens the seashell DANIELLA. I open her door carefully so the sign won't move, and step inside. I don't really know what I'm looking for. Just a clue to explain Daniella's growing pains.

Her room smells like the coconut-mint body spray she's been using since seventh grade. I sift through the clothes on her floor, check the mirror to see if any notes or pictures are torn down. Everything is the same. She has a Quote of the Day calendar on her dresser. It says *Everyone must row with the oars he has.* I look closer and see that it hasn't been changed since July. The whole room is frozen in time. Stuck.

Daniella didn't make her bed before leaving, and the decorative pillows are tossed all over the floor. I think about reassembling them into their usual pyramid. I have her pattern memorized—big striped ones on the bottom, log shapes and circles in the middle, the square sequined one on top. But if I did, she'd know I was in here. Something with sharp blue edges sticks out from underneath her wrinkled bedsheet. It looks like the corner of a book. *It's none of your business,* I think. But deep down I'm desperate to know what she's reading.

"Thoughts" is written in gold on the cover. I open to a page near the front. Daniella's writing, small and precise, fills the page. I drop the diary back onto her bed.

The fuzzy socks are too warm. I start to sweat. If this diary holds the truth, then how can I just stick it back under the sheet? I need to know why my sister has changed, like I know that she keeps sour worms in her sweater drawer.

I pick the diary back up and read.

August 4

I always thought I was this certain kind of person. Someone who wakes up early because they like how mornings feel. A go-getter. Someone who might make history one day.

But something is happening to me. I can feel it. It's like the beginning of a cold but heavier. The only way I can describe it is that once upon a time I had a wall in my chest that surrounded my sadness and kept it contained, and now it's fallen down. Like a Humpty

Dumpty tragic kind of falling down.

Maybe it fell a week ago, the day of high school orientation, when it took me six tries to get my locker open. It really shouldn't have bothered me so much. But every failed try pushed the despair higher up in my chest until my whole heart was infected. The idea of opening this locker for the next four years made me want to drop onto the dirty floor and cry.

Or it might have fallen when we moved Buelo into Kindly Vines. Just me and Mom and Buela. Dad had to work and Mom didn't think Cass should be part of it. I guess fourteen is old enough to be a part of the ugly things. Buelo knocked over the chair in his room, and called Mom and Buela terrible names. He caught my eye in the middle of it, and it was like he'd never seen me in his life. Mom drove slow on the way home and told me what I already knew—Buelo has dementia. His brain has clouded up and made the memories hard to see.

I don't want to think about the way I'm feeling. I want it to go away. So for now I'll just say my wall fell down. And like Humpty

Dumpty, maybe not even the king's horses and men can put it back together again.

Mom drops something metal on the kitchen floor, and I lose the nerve to keep reading. I put the diary back with the corner sticking out from the mess of sheets. My heartbeat thumps, sad and slow. I picture Daniella covered in thin cracks, her growing pains hurting more than any of us realized.

I check her sweater drawer before I leave. I move the cardigans and pullovers around, but there aren't any sour worms in there anymore. If Daniella isn't going to tell me about her high school locker or where she's hiding her candy now, I'm going to have to find out for myself.

And if the king's horses and men can't fix the wall in her chest, then *I'll* do it. Even if I have to keep sneaking into her room to read her diary.

8

Fire + Rain

From the backyard, I can see Daniella's window. She has it cracked and the curtains are open. I sit out by the unlit fire pit in a white plastic chair. The other three chairs are still here from the Chordays' last summer night. My brain burns with an idea.

"Daniella," I call to her window. I know she's in there. She disappeared inside with the door closed after dinner. "Daniella!"

Her face appears, blocked by the screen and framed by banana-yellow curtains.

"What?" she asks.

"Come make a fire with me."

She glances at the pit. I wonder what she thinks about when she looks at the empty chairs. Does she remember the time when Jac scorched her marshmallow and made us all laugh so hard that Ben tipped over onto the grass?

"It's going to rain," she says.

I look up at the sky. No clouds clog up the dim, clear blue.

"It's not raining right now."

"I don't know, Cass."

"Please. We don't have many more weekends until the official end of summer." If I had known that that fire was going to be our last, I never would have put it out. I would have kept feeding it branches and newspaper forever.

"Fine," she says. She disappears from the window. Her bedroom light turns off. A minute later, she comes out the back door wearing jean shorts and a hoodie. She walks barefoot across the deck and onto the grass.

"Did you start?" she asks.

"No, I wanted to wait for you."

She rolls her eyes and picks up some branches from the pile we keep near the pit. I copy her. The wood crisscrosses together on top of burnt ashes, ghosts from summer nights past.

"What's high school like?" I ask, adding a crumpled sheet of newspaper to the pit.

"It's school," Daniella says. She picks up the lighter and holds it close to the wood, just how Dad taught us to. The flame appears and sets a whole stick on fire.

"It has to be a little different. You're my older sister; it's your job to tell me." I take the bottle of lighter fluid and drench the wood in the sharp-smelling liquid. The fire swells.

"Okay, it's a little different." She sits in one of the chairs, and I take the one next to her.

"We could talk about it, you know. Or we can talk about anything you want to," I say.

She turns to me. The fire lights up half her face. For a second I think she might tell me about the wall in her chest, or her high school orientation, or that moving Buelo to Kindly Vines changed something inside her.

"How's Jac and Ben?"

"Jac is Jac. Ben's already talking about the spring musical."

I think she might smile a little, but it's hard to tell in the dusky light.

"Of course he is," she says.

"I know they want to hang out with you. The four of us. Like always." I try to keep my voice even. Casual. Everything can be normal if I just act normal. I'm still Cassi and she's still Daniella and we're still the Chordays.

"I've been busy. I have . . . more homework now."

How much homework could she have one week into the school year? The truth is as bright as the flames. She's not going to tell me anything. I stare at the fire until my eyes hurt. When I look away, I see dark spots. No, they're real spots. Wet spots.

"I knew it was going to rain," Daniella says.

The rain comes down, persistent but too light to put the fire out completely. Daniella runs to the hose and fills a bucket with water. She comes back over to dump the bucket onto the wood. Smoke shoots up into the storm. Daniella tosses the bucket away and sprints inside just as the rain starts to pour. I'm right behind her, thinking about how fast the sky can switch from blue to gray.

"Sorry," I say when we reach the kitchen. I close the screen door.

I want us to collapse into a pile of laughter, the way we used to when summer showers caught us by surprise. I want us to dry our hair with the dishtowels next to the sink.

"I don't think you've been rained on enough," she said, and squeezed her T-shirt out onto my arms.

"I have, I have," I cried, almost choking on giddiness.

"Whatever, Cassi."

Daniella's voice sounds like it did at Kindly Vines. Like she's accusing me of something. She walks out of the kitchen, leaving watery footprints and loose blades of grass and me behind.

9

Nachos

Making nachos requires a careful system. I spread the chips, Jac sprinkles the cheese on top, and Ben mans the microwave to make sure the cheese fully melts. There was a fourth piece to the process when Daniella would hang out with us. She handled the toppings, since she could chop onions without crying. Ben does it now.

"Is that a fourth handful?" I ask. Jac's hand is in the plastic bag of shredded cheddar.

"I lost count." She grins.

"Three handfuls, Jac. Otherwise the chip-to-cheese ratio is compromised."

"Live a little." She spreads the most-likely-fourth handful over the tortilla chips.

Ben dumps the tomatoes and onions and jalapeños on top and then sticks the plate into the microwave. He tap-dances in his socks on the kitchen tiles while the timer ticks down. I can't help but notice how his face is an even blend of his parents, who are both Korean. Jac imitates taking pictures of him like a celebrity photographer. She crouches and then hops onto the counter.

Nachos

"Why didn't you ever come back to the floor?" Ben asked while we walked to Mrs. Chay's station wagon after the *Welcome to Middle School* dance. He cha-cha'd across the sidewalk, like there was still music playing in his head. Jac pretended to shake maracas.

I didn't want to say that it felt hard to be myself, when it seemed like the easiest thing in the world for them.

"The fruit punch had real fruit in it," I answered.

Maybe everyone's sets of facts about their friends have missing pieces. Some things you just keep to yourself.

The microwave beeps. Ben pulls the plate out and sets it on the counter.

"Definitely more than three handfuls," he says. There's so much cheese, you can't even see the chips. The nachos are like me. The ratio is off.

We take our food to the living room and eat on the floor. Jac starts the next episode of a documentary series we've been watching about people who've had real encounters with ghosts. The orchard owners in the last episode could tell the ghost was around when they started to smell oranges, because oranges weren't able to grow at the orchard anymore. I slept with the light on for a week and haven't eaten an orange since.

"I tried to help Daniella," I say over the creepy intro music.

"How?" Ben asks. He shrugs his shoulders a bunch of times.

"I re-created a classic Chorday memory. Backyard bonfire."

We stare at the plate of nachos like we've all just remembered who was supposed to chop the onions.

"Did it work? Was she . . . like herself again?" Jac asks.

"It started raining."

Ben's head pops up. He has his about-to-sing face on.

"That memory isn't even the best one." Each word in his sentence goes up an octave. "There's tons of others to re-create." He reaches his falsetto. Jac covers her ears.

"Like what?" I ask, ready to add to my list of ways to bring Daniella back.

"Watching the Founders' Day fireworks on the hill outside." Ben switches back to speaking. He pries Jac's palms off her face. "You love my singing."

I think about the fireworks last June. I sat between Jac and Ben on Jac's camouflage comforter. Daniella laid with her head in my lap while I tied sections of her hair into braids.

"That's a good one," I say. "Except I don't really have access to fireworks on a daily basis."

"Doing our skits at the library Open Mic night?" Ben suggests.

Mom runs the Open Mic night at the library every fall. The Chordays always perform. Ben writes our skits and types them up on professional-looking paper. Sometimes they're so funny, we end up laughing too hard to finish. Sometimes they're serious, like last year's. Ben wrote about a character who'd been trapped in a locker, and the people the character saw and the things he overheard while stuck inside. Ben played the one in the locker. The rest of us played the people who didn't stop to help him.

We were quiet after that skit.

"Much better," I say. "Make sure you have a skit ready to go for this year?"

"On it." He puts his hands under his chin and squints like he's already thinking hard about plots and dialogue.

"I got one! The day we signed our names on my wall in permanent marker," Jac adds.

Ben and I look at her.

"We were grounded for that," I say.

"Though I still don't understand how your dad had the power to ground all of us," Ben adds.

Jac smiles. The TV behind her zooms in on a picture of a skull.

"Rebellion makes me feel alive." Her ponytail tips to the side, a bright blue reminder of that fact.

We get quiet and turn back to the documentary, like listing memories has worn us out. The story behind the episode begins: A cobbler is being haunted by a customer who died while buying boots. The show is done with reenactments and bad animation, but the ghosts still stick in my mind for days.

"I thought a cobbler was a fruit-filled dessert," Jac says.

"It's a shoemaker, too," I tell her.

"This acting is terrible," Ben says, but his voice is a shaky whisper.

The front door opens.

Ben screams, and it echoes through the whole town house. Uncle Eric stands at the entrance.

"Nice to see you too, Ben." He steps inside. A woman in tight jeans and high-heeled boots follows behind him, holding a giant teddy bear. Jac makes a growling sound in her throat.

The cobbler goes down to the basement of his shop. Everyone knows you should *never* go into a basement if you suspect a haunting.

"I want to introduce you to Leslie." Uncle Eric waves an arm in front of his date like she's a fancy product on a shopping network. "The carnival is awesome this year, you three. I'll take you tomorrow if you want to go."

"And I'd love to go again." Leslie's voice is kind; her eyes are on Jac.

"No, thanks." Jac is still facing the TV.

The basement door slams behind the cobbler even though no one pushed it. I flinch.

"Maybe another time." Leslie shifts her focus to the teddy bear. It has a red bow tie sewn into its neck.

Ben and I look at each other. Jac can make this

moment awkward to the power of ten. She's done it before—to Shauna and Corrine and Kerry and everyone else Uncle Eric has dated since separating from Jac's mom last year. Jac spends most of her time at Uncle Eric's since it's closer to school, and the rest of her time at her mom's new house in the next town over. Mom said that when two people meet in high school like Uncle Eric and Jac's mom did, they sometimes drift apart from one another. It confused me, because I knew that Mom and Dad had met in high school too. I wondered why some people stayed together, and others split apart.

"Probably not. In fact, I will probably never see you again." She looks at Uncle Eric. "Right, Dad?"

The cobbler tries to escape but the door is locked. Uncle Eric runs a hand over his bald head.

"Jac was born with a wonderful sense of humor," he adds, and guides Leslie to the door. "Let me walk you out."

I think she whispers good-bye. I can faintly hear her heels tap down the brick front steps.

"That was a hot mess." Ben snaps his fingers.

"*You're* a hot mess." Jac bends her legs up to her chest and rests her chin on her knees. Her eyes stay glued to the TV screen, like there aren't rivers of blood leaking down the basement steps. I'll be sleeping with the light on tonight.

Uncle Eric comes back. He looks much less cheerful this time. He walks over to the TV and shuts it off.

"Are you happy with yourself?" he asks, staring pointedly at Jac.

"Thrilled," she answers.

"Rude is not a good look on you. Neither is that hair. You told me the blue would be gone by now." Uncle Eric points to his own head, which doesn't make much sense because of the being-bald thing.

Jac's hair does look darker than it did at yoga, a blue like the sky just before the sun comes up.

"I don't know how dye works, Dad. I'm not a chemist."

"Well, become one. And fast. Or we'll march straight down to Cost Cutters and ask them for a nice buzz cut."

Daniella should be sprawled out on the carpet with us. She'd run a hand down Jac's spine and calm down the fight, press her forehead into Jac's and whisper *Don't get so mad* the way she used to.

"You wouldn't," Jac says.

"I would. I'm not doing this with you anymore." Uncle Eric points back and forth between the two of them and then walks out of the room.

We stare at the black screen in silence. Eventually Ben reaches down to the nacho plate and tosses a tomato chunk at Jac. She only half smiles, but it's entirely genuine.

"You'd look good with a buzz cut," I say, because if I

tried to put my forehead on Jac's, she would probably head-butt me. I can't replace Daniella.

"If I go down, you're going down with me." She turns the documentary back on.

10

North Sapling

Mr. G has another lesson on the whiteboard. *Lesson Two of Math Olympics: Identify useful patterns. They can show you what comes next. Those tricky future-tellers.* I write the words in my notebook and then scribble until the class fills.

"Cool drawings." Aaron takes the seat in front of me. He dumps his backpack onto the ground.

"They're just doodles." I cover up my paper with my arm.

"Still. It's interesting to see how your mind works."

I'm not sure how lightning bolts and curlicues show how my mind works. The best part of doodling is that I don't have to think at all.

Mr. G closes the door. His tie looks like a pencil. He circles the room with a stack of papers and places one on each of our desks.

"We have to be ready for anything on the assessments. Complete this practice test, if you dare." He laughs like the villain in a cartoon. I imagine him as a dark-cloaked vampire, teaching us to suck blood instead of simplify fractions.

"Can we work with a partner?" Sage asks, already scooting her desk closer to Allie's.

"As long as you know that you'll have to work on your own on the actual assessments." He doesn't sound cartoonish anymore. I identify the useful pattern of Mr. G. *No villain voice = Being serious.*

Aaron keeps his head bowed over his paper, like he has no plans to tell me a tree town story, but that's fine. I never said I wanted to hear them anyway. I focus on the first question.

Find the total surface area of a rectangular prism with the measurements 5 ft x 3 ft x 2 ft.

My eyes dart to the drawings in my notebook. I spot the rectangular prisms that I sketched and shaded in. If doodles reflect a mind the way Aaron says, then my mind works in math problems. I add *mildly insightful* to my set of Aaron Facts.

"Did you get the right answer?" Aaron turns around in his chair.

"It's hard to know for sure," I say.

"There's an answer key." He shows me. The answers are printed small and upside down on the back of the practice assessment. I can make out *#1: 62 square feet*, which is what I wrote on my paper.

"Some people call that cheating," I say.

Aaron draws thick, hard lines across the answers.

"There. Can't have anyone thinking I'm a cheater." He blows off the graphite dust.

I think about things that don't have answer keys on

the back. Diaries. Nightmares. Job applications like the one my Life Skills teacher, Mrs. Barnes, had us fill out for homework last year.

The first part wasn't so hard. I just had to put my name and address and previous employment. Mrs. Barnes said we could make jobs up for that part, so I wrote "Mathematician," "Nacho Maker," and "Owner of a Bird Sanctuary."

But the last section asked me to self-identify. Are you Hispanic or Latino—yes or no? *I checked the box for yes, and then read on.* If yes, do not continue.

I continued anyway.

The items in the next list confused me. Caucasian (Not Hispanic or Latino). *Mom found me at the kitchen table, my pencil hovering over the paper. I asked her why the application said I couldn't be both when I knew I was. She touched my hair.*

"These things are complicated, mi amor. *But I want you to never forget two things. One, the privilege you have because of your dad, and two, the place your mom comes from," she said.*

I told myself that I wouldn't forget. I checked the Caucasian (Not Hispanic or Latino) *box too. Two check marks to show both sides of me, even if it didn't feel quite right. Mrs. Barnes took off five points and wrote "Please follow instructions" in the application's margins.*

"Have you ever heard of North Sapling, New York?" Aaron asks.

His voice interrupts my thinking about checkboxes telling me who I am.

"No," I answer.

"They're known for being environmentally conscious. The whole place gets together to plant a community garden. It was our first tree town, three years ago."

Curiosity creeps up on me. I look up from the practice assessment.

"What did you plant?"

"Myself." Aaron grins.

"What?" I imagine Aaron growing out of a rosebush, or sprouting from a root like a potato.

"The problem was that we moved there in the winter. Plants can't grow too well then." He spins his pencil between his fingers.

"But people can?"

"People can grow at any time. I grew a foot in one summer."

His pencil keeps spinning. I count the different ways people can grow. *Out of something. Up. Apart.*

"So your story is that you got taller," I say.

I think about those memes on the internet, the ones that compare what you think is going to happen to what actually happens. I apply the pattern to my deal with Aaron like I'm plugging *x* into an equation.

Expectation: Stories like the ones Buelo told when he

still lived in the condo on Smith Street, about beaches at night and fireflies in jars. His Eduardo Story.

Reality: A story about growing a few inches.

Aaron takes a breath like he's not finished.

"I decided to go to one of the gardens anyway. Frost covered the whole thing. I walked down the rows where the vegetables were supposed to grow, like I was planting my own footsteps. I thought someone should put one of those little paper labels next to them. You know, the ones that show you what's going to grow? It would let people know that Aaron's Boot Prints were there. Maybe there would even be a scientific name, like *Bootus printus* or something."

Aaron's sentences build and build like cake layers.

"Then what?" I ask, leaning closer, on the edge of my seat.

"I ran back to—"

"How's it going over here?" Mr. G points his pencil tie to the practice assessment on my desk. I forgot it was there.

"The first one is sixty-two square feet," I answer.

"And the second?"

"To be determined," Aaron says.

"I love a good work in progress. But let's keep it moving." He waves the end of his pencil tie like he's writing something in the air. We nod at him.

Aaron pushes his desk back so it's next to mine. I

stare at the assessment. Half my mind is on the second problem, and the other half is on Aaron's story.

The problem asks me to find how much profit Janelle's Cookie Barn made last year.

Step one: Figure out how much Janelle's Cookie Barn spent.

What else happened in the garden?

"I ran back to our rental house and took some things from my room. Like the shoe from my Monopoly game and a Superman comic book." Aaron works on the problem while he talks. "My footsteps were still in the garden when I got back. I dug into each imprint and put my stuff in the holes, then covered it back up."

Step two: Find out how much Janelle's Cookie Barn made.

What would I plant myself with?

"I like to think about someone finding it all when the weather got warm and they were ready to grow a new crop of plants. And then they'd know who I was back then."

Step three: Subtract the initial cost from the total sales.

A calculator or my pebble CASSANDRA *sign or a red chili from Pepper's Pizza.*

"Who were you?" I ask.

Aaron presses his pencil into the assessment a little too hard. Pieces of the tip crumble off.

"I was nine. I'm not that into Superman anymore."

Aaron slides his paper toward me so we can compare, his face a little pink. We got the same result. I flip the assessment over to check the answer key.

"We were right," I say, and look at Aaron. He draws shapes that look like shields on his paper. He's right. It is interesting to see the way his mind works. I add *tells good stories* to my set of Aaron Facts.

Before I can think too hard about it, I stick my hand out toward him.

"I accept your deal. One story from every tree town."

Aaron lifts his head, and his long hair flops to the side.

"Excellent," he says.

His hand wraps around mine. We shake once, twice, three times. When I let go, it feels like something warm and permanent is left on my skin.

We're both smiling when we move on to the next problem.

September 12

High school smells like sweat covered in lavender perfume. Like a humid, smothering blanket so thick that I can't breathe. But I don't think it smells like that for everyone.

To Jenna I think it might smell like McIntosh apples, new denim, and cracked-open books. I think Mason, who I technically dated for two months last year even though we barely talked, who is only a freshman and already a star on the football team, might smell fresh cut grass and chilly nights and that black goo the players smear on their faces.

There was a pep rally today. I don't have a drop of pep in me. The football team flexed their muscles and wore orange jerseys. The cheerleaders demanded we give them an *M* for "Mapleton." I just couldn't. Jenna nudged me and asked, "Are you okay?"

But what if the answer is "Yes and no"? Or

"I don't think you'd understand if I told you, because I don't really even understand"? Or "I don't know, but I'm pretty sure this gym is going to devour me and spit my bones out later"?

11

Tired

Dad owns a sandwich shop with Uncle Eric called Holy Baloney. One Thursday a month he leaves before the dinner rush to visit Buelo with Daniella and me. He makes sure to walk through our front door at exactly four p.m. with three chicken salad sandwiches. We call it Dad-Visit Thursday.

It's 3:50 p.m. My heart pounds and my palms leave sweat marks on the parrot place mat. I haven't been to Kindly Vines since Daniella said those things. I imagine walking to room 201, the walls whispering at me. *It must be weird for you. You're always like* that. *That, that, that.*

Daniella comes into the kitchen. Her hair is a dark, snarly mess. Mascara crumbles stick to her cheeks like black constellations.

"Tell Dad I'm not going," she says. She walks over to the refrigerator.

"Why not?" I ask.

Daniella stares into the white refrigerator light.

"I'm tired."

I want her to sit at the kitchen table in front of the toucan place mat. I want to tell her about Aaron's tree town story. I want Dad to walk through the door with our chicken salad sandwiches wrapped in parchment paper.

"I could make you coffee. Buela showed me how."

Daniella shuts the refrigerator. The glass jars on the door rattle.

"It's not that hard," she says, and walks out of the kitchen so fast that it's like she was never here. I listen to her footsteps on the stairs, in the hallway between our bedrooms. I want to mute all the sounds so I won't hear her door close.

"Yes it is," I whisper to the parrot.

Dad and I sit next to each other and eat our grinders without saying much. He put Daniella's in the fridge for her to find later. I bet the bread is already soggy.

"What did she say when you talked to her?" I ask. Dad balls a napkin up in his hand. He sits at the oriole place mat wearing his black polo with "Holy Baloney" stitched into the top right corner, the same as any other Dad-Visit Thursday. But Daniella isn't here to split the bag of salt-and-vinegar chips with him.

"She had a long day at school. A lot of quizzes. She just needs to rest." He takes a handful of chips. Does he think about Daniella when he looks at the blue bag?

Tired

Does he feel her absence like a bruise the way I do when I listen to our favorite songs alone?

"I think she'd feel better if she just came downstairs and ate sandwiches with us," I reply.

"Maybe. But that's not what she wants to do today. Starting high school is tough. Your sister is dealing with it in her own way," he says.

According to her diary, it's not that simple. Clammy smells and carnivorous gyms are involved. But Daniella can't find out that I've been sneaking into her room.

"Middle school is tough too," I mumble.

Dad taps his knuckle against mine.

"You're right, Cassi. I didn't mean it like that."

I tap Dad's knuckle back. People always tell me I look like him. We both have the same square faces and round noses, eyes the color of clovers.

"I'm just worried, that's all," I say.

"She'll be fine. It's a matter of adjusting." Dad crunches up our mayonnaise-stained parchment paper. "Let's head out. Your mom should be there soon."

We always meet Mom at Kindly Vines on Dad-Visit Thursdays, after she's finished running a crime-novel club at the library. I pick up the dirty utensils, the mayonnaise packets, the salt-and-vinegar chips. Some leftovers crunch inside the bag. I may look like Dad, but I don't like salt-and-vinegar chips. He only shares that with Daniella.

The phone rings. Dad answers before I can check the caller ID.

"Everything okay?" he asks instead of saying hello.

Dad listens. I can't hear a thing. The oriole has a chunk of chicken salad on its feathers.

"Are you sure you don't want us to come?"

I swipe the chicken salad off. It leaves a pale streak.

"Okay. See you when you get home. Love you." Dad hangs up.

"We're not going?" I ask. Dad stares at the phone like the buttons might answer my question.

"Your Buelo is tired." Dad's voice stumbles over Spanish words the way mine does. He finally looks up. "We'll go see him another time. Soon."

The look on Dad's face + not being able to see Buelo = Another bad day, like the one that made Buelo go to Kindly Vines in the first place.

"Fine. I'll do my homework," I say, and leave the kitchen.

It's silent behind Daniella's door when I walk by. She's tired, Buelo's tired. Maybe everyone should get a good night's sleep and everything will go back to normal.

12

Electricity

Daniella's eighth-grade graduation was on the high school football field. Chairs for the graduates were set up in perfect rows, right on top of the Mustang mascot painted on the center of the field. It looked like it was running away.

The day was warm, and the sun spilled all over the bleachers where we sat. I was between Mom and Buelo. Buelo's cane was shiny and silver in the light, glaring at me. He had started using it a few months before, after he'd fallen down in the condo's steep driveway on his way to get the mail.

Buela was next to Mom, scrolling on her phone. Sometimes I thought Buela was better with phones than I was. She was always posting inspirational quotes and videos of yawning puppies. I did like the sleepy baby dogs.

"I got an update from Celina today. The electricity at her house is still spotty." She showed Mom the message on the screen. Titi Celina was my grandaunt, Buelo's sister. She sent me a little figurine every year for my birthday.

"It's been months," Mom said, shaking her head.

When Titi Celina's town was hit hard by a hurricane,

it took weeks for us to hear that she was okay. Buela and Buelo didn't do much during that time but pray and watch the news. Sometimes I'd watch with them and see the places we'd visited, destroyed by water and wind.

Buela and Mom kept talking about the state of the island. I looked at Buelo. He was wearing his brown jacket and hat because he got cold even in June, plus he liked to look nice when he went out. His wrinkled hands were folded on top of his cane.

"Are you feeling okay, Buelo?" I asked.

He'd been quiet on the drive to the high school, and lately. Ever since his fall. I couldn't remember the last time he'd told me a story.

"Sí, corazón."

I winced. "Corazón" was what he called Mom. I was supposed to be his corazónita.

The band started playing the graduation song, and the eighth-grade class walked out the doors of the gym in their royal-blue caps and gowns. I spotted Daniella near the front of the line with Jenna. They laughed and waved to the crowd like queens. Daniella had straightened her hair for the ceremony. Mom raised her camera and took pictures when she passed by.

Everyone sat down, and I lost Daniella in the rows of graduation caps. The principal talked about moving on and facing the world and taking with you the lessons learned along the way. Panic swept over me. I couldn't find Daniella.

Electricity

She'd be in high school next year. She was moving on.

The superintendent called the eighth graders up one by one to get their certificates.

"Daniella Celina Chord," she read into a microphone.

We stood and clapped while Daniella crossed the stage, squinting into the sun. She wore high-heeled wedges that laced up her shins. When the superintendent handed her the certificate, Daniella lifted it over her head and shook her hips back and forth. Her straightened hair swayed. It reminded me of the way she'd danced in the center of the floor at Buelo and Buela's fiftieth anniversary party, or how she sometimes danced all by herself, singing along with the songs in Spanish.

"She has the fire, that one," Buela said to Mom.

"Woo-hoo!"

I turned, and Buelo was on his feet cheering. He didn't hold on to his cane, and his smile went all the way to his eyes. That was all I needed to convince me that things would be fine. Daniella bounced back into her seat. Now I knew exactly where she was.

After the ceremony, everyone gathered in the area outside the cafeteria to take pictures. Part of the cafeteria jutted out from the rest of the building, encased in glass, so it looked like a greenhouse. You could see right through the walls.

"There she is," Dad said. He wrapped an arm around Daniella when she stepped into our circle. Mom snapped another picture. Then another when Buela kissed Daniella on the cheek, and when Daniella took the cap off her head and put it on me. I hung the picture up in my room. We both had our sister smiles on.

"Where's Buelo?" Daniella asked. Mom snapped another picture then, right at the moment when we all realized Buelo wasn't in the circle with us anymore. I looked at that picture later too. Dad had an urgent look on his face, and Buela had a hand over her mouth. Daniella's eyes were closed. The only part of me in the picture was my hand, nails painted robin's-egg blue.

"Spread out," Dad said quietly.

Buela inched through the crowd saying, "Pico, Pico." Dad headed for the woods on the other side of the field. I went toward the benches near the glass part of the cafeteria, because if there was anything that I knew about my Buelo, it was that he liked a good bench to sit on.

But the benches were empty. I looked to the transparent wall. At first, all I saw was my reflection, my pink sundress and the graduation cap slipping off my head. Then I looked closer and saw Buelo. The tables in the cafeteria were folded up and pushed to the side, so he stood in the middle of the bare floor.

I ran around the glass section and through the door. Buelo had his face tilted up to the ceiling, but that wasn't what made me stop short. He held his worn, brown wallet above his head, like he was offering cash to the ceiling lights. I stepped closer.

Electricity

"Buelo, what are you doing?" My voice sounded like a breath.

"Catching it," Buelo answered. He opened up his wallet and stretched out the part where dollar bills go.

"Catching what?" I heard footsteps behind me. Then the rest of my family was at my side. Buelo's cane rested next to him, watching the whole scene like a witness.

"Electricity. For Celina." He lowered the wallet and tucked it back into his pocket. "We will send to her."

Mom rushed up to him. She took Buelo's arm and guided him over to us.

"Okay, Papi, we'll send it to her."

We all went back outside, but no one said anything about taking more pictures. Or about what had just happened with Buelo. We left the high school to meet Jac and Ben and Uncle Eric and the Chays at the graduation party they had set up for Daniella at the picnic tables behind Lakeside Townhouses. I kept my arm around Buelo's on the drive over. Even if the logical part of my brain knew that Buelo couldn't catch electricity in his wallet, another part understood why he'd try. I'd do anything for my sister too.

Mom made the call to Kindly Vines the next morning when she thought we were asleep. Buelo went to live there twenty-nine days later, the same time Daniella started closing her door and stopped being a member of the Chordays.

Autumn

13

Open Mic

I sit at the sign-up table with Daniella on Open Mic night at the library. The event is in the back corner where the young adult books are shelved. Earlier, we helped Mom drag the circle tables out and replace them with metal folding chairs for the audience. The refreshments were off to the side. Soon the table would be covered in trays of sandwiches from Holy Baloney, cut into triangles.

Daniella didn't complain once. Not even when Mom made us wipe the dusty chairs down with lemon bleach. She's still quiet now sitting next to me, chewing on the end of a pen. Her hair is half pulled up and half loose. She's wearing a big blue sweatshirt and black leggings with a hole in the knee.

"Are you excited?" I ask.

It feels like it takes her a whole night to turn and look at me.

"For what?"

"It's Open Mic night. We love Open Mic night."

I look to the door. Now would be a good moment for

Ben to rush in with a stack of scripts still hot from the printer. We could gather in the upstairs area of the non-fiction section, the way we always do. Daniella used to alternate between focusing on our makeshift rehearsals and running her hands over the biographies of historical figures.

"Did you know that Joan of Arc was only a teenager when she went to battle?" she asked when we were practicing last year's skit with the locker.

"Wow," I said, because the Joan of Arc fact was interesting and because sometimes it felt like Daniella knew everything.

"Did you know that there's only twenty minutes until curtain?" Ben shook his script in the air.

"Easy, Ben. You're entering diva territory. What will the tabloids say?" But Daniella came and sat back down because she knew how important our skits were to him.

"I'm not performing," Daniella says.

The vents above us blast out a wave of cold air. A chill shoots up my spine.

"Ben is writing a skit for us," I say.

"I'm just here for the community service hours. I have to do eighty before I graduate."

I saw a pamphlet about that in the stack of papers Daniella had dumped on the kitchen counter after her orientation. It was called *Learning Through Service*. The student on the front of the pamphlet was knee-deep in a brown lake with a net in his hand, scooping trash out of the water.

"Can't acting be community service?"

I'm joking, but Daniella doesn't laugh.

"Come on, Cass. I'm tired."

You are not tired. You look sad. *And how will you ever feel better if you don't just do this skit like normal?*

The door opens and Dad comes in with a big silver tray in his arms. Uncle Eric follows behind with another tray, and then Leslie steps in with a bucket of chips. Maybe I could hold the salt-and-vinegar chips hostage until Daniella decides to perform with us. Maybe she doesn't even like chips anymore.

"Another one?" Daniella mumbles under her breath. I assume she's talking about Uncle Eric's new friend.

"Her name is Leslie. He took her to the carnival. Jac and Uncle Eric got into a huge fight when he introduced us." I fill her in on what she's missed, whether she wants to hear it or not.

Daniella nods, killing the conversation, but it doesn't matter because we're not alone anymore. Uncle Eric and Leslie set the food down and come to the sign-up area.

"No names yet," Uncle Eric says.

"It's early," I say. "Where's Jac?"

"She said she had to do something with Ben. She'll come with the Chays."

Daniella puts a hand on either side of her face and leans onto her elbows on the table, closing her eyes. Leslie watches her like she's studying a painting. Uncle Eric rubs his head.

"Paul! Eric! I need help with the speaker," Mom calls from the performance area. She's unraveling a knotted ball of wires. Uncle Eric and Dad rush over. Leslie stays at the sign-up area, still watching Daniella.

"I'm Leslie. Are you feeling okay?" she asks. Daniella raises her head. Her bottom lip is swollen from her chewing on it. The dark circles under her eyes look like she either smeared her mascara or hasn't slept in days.

"Excuse me." Daniella stands up from the chair and it groans. She walks away, to the stairs that lead up to the biographies, a swirl of dark hair and baggy clothes.

She's just going to read about Joan of Arc, I think. Or Queen Elizabeth or Jackie Robinson or Aristotle.

"Is she all right?" Leslie asks.

"Yes. She's upset that she has to do community service."

A woman with long white hair and a tambourine stands behind Leslie.

"Can I sign up?" she asks.

I nod at her and Leslie steps away. She starts to spread the bags of chips out on the table. The tambourine woman writes "Helen, musical adventurer" on the sheet, and I wish, for the trillionth time since fall started, that Daniella were here with me. Even if she's in a bad mood.

The sign-up sheet is half-full of poets and singers when Jac and Ben show up with the Chays. Jac's hair is wet and slicked against her face. They meet me at the table.

"Jac, you look . . . damp?" I say. She shakes her head, and some liquid lands on my arm. The mark it leaves is deep blue, like some of the Kool-Aid is seeping out, but the color of her hair looks darker now somehow. Whatever article she read about Kool-Aid dye was seriously misinformed.

"Ben said I could be a sea monster in the skit," she explains.

"No. What I said was that it was going to ruin the integrity of the scene, but you said I had no choice, so here we are." Ben hands me a script.

Title: Midnight Madness. Characters: Four moviegoers in line for a sold-out midnight premiere who were all accidently booked for the same seat. Chaos ensues.

"It sounds amazing, Ben," I say, and I mean it. Sometimes I wonder how Ben's head isn't bigger, since it's full of so many ideas.

"It's a masterpiece," Mr. Chay says. He wears khaki pants and a Mapleton Community Theater shirt. He has about ten of them. One for every summer Ben has been doing plays there.

"Smile!" Mrs. Chay pops up in front of us with

her camera. She takes a camera everywhere, partially because she's a professional photographer and partially because of her favorite saying—"Every opportunity is a photo opportunity." The camera is wrapped around her neck with a band that says *Ben's Mom.*

Other than Jac and me, Ben's parents are his biggest fans.

Jac does her signature smile, and the air from the vents turns to ice. Ben wraps one arm around each of our shoulders. Mrs. Chay snaps the picture, then spins the camera around so we can see it.

"I'll print it for you all," Mrs. Chay says. She and Mr. Chay go over to help my parents at the refreshment table. I spot the big container of kimchi Mrs. Chay offered to bring as a sandwich topping. Kimchi tastes good with just about everything. Dad and Uncle Eric even made a special sandwich at Holy Baloney to use it on—the Kim-Chay.

I watch them each shake Leslie's hand. Jac gnashes her teeth like a wolf.

"Re-lax," Ben says. He taps her on the arm with his scripts.

"He's supposed to be done with her by now. Her two-week time limit is up."

"Maybe she's different," I say. I mean, everything else is. Daniella isn't in Mrs. Chay's annual Open Mic picture.

"Not helpful."

A mime with his face painted white comes over to sign up. I'd be startled, but all kinds of acts come to perform at Open Mic. When he walks, silently, to take a seat, Ben picks up the pen and writes the title of the skit and our names.

"You can take Daniella off," I say. Ben pauses in the middle of his own name. *Be.*

"Why? Where is she?" Jac asks.

I point toward the stairs to the nonfiction section. The stairs we should be scrambling up in order to rehearse right now.

"The skit won't work without four people," Ben says. His voice is panicked.

"Sorry, Ben."

"I'll talk to her." He sticks what should be Daniella's script under his arm and heads for the stairs.

"No. She's . . ." I mean to say "tired," but Ben's already out of reach. He climbs up toward Daniella and Joan of Arc.

I feel a tap on my shoulder. Jac and I turn around, and Leslie is there.

"I'd love to fill in for your skit. I did some theater in college."

Jac starts to fake cough into her hand.

"I can't perform either," she rasps. "I'm sick."

She steals a pen from the sign-in table and goes to

sit in one of the chairs, arms crossed. Ben comes back downstairs. He still has Daniella's script.

"The show must go on," he says. He crosses out "Midnight Madness" and all our names except his.

The people and shelves of books around me go fuzzy, like none of this is real. I'm in a bad dream. That must be it. I close my eyes hard like I do when I'm trying to wake up from a nightmare, then open them again. I'm still here.

"We're going to get started," Mom says from the performance area behind us. She got the wires untangled. The audience settles into their seats with their props and cheese sandwiches. I sit between Jac and Ben. Daniella doesn't come down. Mom starts calling performers up one by one, and when they're done, Jac writes a score on the back of her script, even though you're not supposed to judge at Open Mic night. She gives Helen, musical adventurer, a five. She gives the mime a negative three.

"Ben Chay." Mom claps like she does when she introduces everyone. Mrs. Chay stands and takes what sounds like twenty pictures. Mr. Chay points to his Mapleton Community Theater shirt. Ben stands at the microphone.

"I'll be performing a monologue," he says. The feeling I get when I watch all his plays washes over me. Nervousness for him. Pride that he's my best friend.

"I remember the time I went swimming in the ocean

in April. The water was cold enough to freeze the world, to make me feel more alive than ever before. I decided I liked the cold water enough to put it on my list of favorite things—in between dress rehearsals and the smell of wet sidewalks. Above pumpkin lattes—decaf, Mom, I promise."

He gets a few muffled laughs for that one. Mrs. Chay looks like she might weep. I hear soft footsteps on the stairs and turn around. Daniella is there, watching.

"The following April I went back to the ocean. I couldn't wait for the sharp, exhilarating chill of cold water. To feel big and small at the same time. To feel like everything I'd ever been through was important. But it didn't feel the same. I don't know why. It's possible there are some moments that you only get to have once."

The audience is quiet now. I feel tears in my throat— the scared, helpless kind. What if we only get to be the Chordays once, and now it's over?

"Thank you," Ben says. He walks off to the sound of applause, the loudest of all the performers that night.

"Encore, encore," Dad and Uncle Eric call out from the refreshment table, clapping their rubber-gloved hands. Ben bows at them. He sits back in his seat, his face flushed, his breath heavy. I turn around. Daniella is gone.

"What did you think?" Ben asks.

Jac taps her pen thoughtfully against her cheek, then writes his score under the others.

"I never thought I'd do this," she says.

She flips the script so he can see it.

It says ten.

September 21

I've been thinking a lot about when I was a Girl
Scout. Mom would park the car and walk me
inside, her troop leader bag banging between
us. On our way through the hallways, I would
imagine myself at fourteen, smiling, spinning a
locker dial and eagerly making it to class just as
the bell was ringing.

Wednesdays at six thirty p.m. in the home
economics room at the high school, my troop
mates and I pledged to be honest and brave
and true. Jenna was in my troop. Back then, the
boys in our fifth-grade class called her a rag doll
because of her cherry-colored hair and how quiet
she was. When we all recited our pledge, three
fingers raised to the fluorescent tubes of light,
Jenna barely whispered.

She's grown out of that now.

I remember one meeting when Mom
announced the prizes that everyone had won for
selling cookies. Jenna won a set of satin pajamas.

The runner-up won a case of goopy lip gloss. My heart ran ragged and my palms got all damp like I'd plopped them into a pool. I was the only one who hadn't gotten a prize yet.

"Daniella sold the most cookies and wins the wheelie sneakers," Mom said. The troop handed the shoebox along until it dropped into my lap like an anchor.

This girl named Kylie, who moved away before middle school, told Mom that it wasn't fair I'd won the wheelie sneakers, since I was the troop leader's daughter. I wiped my hands on my green sash and looked down at the badges sewn onto it. I didn't ask to be the troop leader's daughter, or to win the wheelie sneakers. I didn't even want wheelie sneakers. I wanted to wear high heels, and be in high school, and have a locker.

"Daniella worked hard to sell her cookies. She went door-to-door through the whole neighborhood," Mom said.

"My mom said it's not safe to go door-to-door," Kylie argued back.

"It is if you have an adult with you."

"My mom's too busy."

"I'm sorry you're disappointed, Kylie. But you're all getting cookie badges, and that's what counts."

"Get into your craft groups, everyone," Jenna's mom, the assistant leader, called out. The troop divided. I broke free to the bathroom across the hall, just to get away from Kylie's glares.

I loved the sensors on the sinks, the tiles on the floor. I wanted it all to be mine. I wanted to be old enough to use the tampon dispenser. In fifth grade the bathroom was still in my classroom, but in high school it was an island, it was alone time, it was all grown up.

Now I'm the age I wanted to be back then. I go to that high school. And half the time, the sensors on those sinks don't even work.

14

Fairy Tales

It's dark. I can hear moving water out there somewhere. I follow the sound until my bare feet sink into cold sand.

The dark lake in front of me stirs, and something rises like a sea monster. Daniella. Striped with seaweed and wearing a quinceañera dress, like Hispanic girls do for their fifteenth birthdays. But Daniella is only fourteen.

She sits cross-legged in front of me. A scream lodges in my throat, threatening to explode. Broken bottles and chip bags float around in the lake behind her.

"Will we ever be the same again?" I whisper. Her dress is crusted in sludge, spread out like a fan, as dark as the water. It's big and blue like Cinderella's. She reaches out her arm, covered in deep-green algae.

I follow her finger to the center of my chest. I'm wearing a quinceañera dress too, pink like Sleeping Beauty's. It's sandy and soaked through to my skin. Itchy fabric hangs off my shoulders. The top part is too big for my body. I'm further from my quinceañera than Daniella. Further from Daniella than I've ever been.

Wake up, wake up, wake up.

My eyes open. I brush away the sweaty hair stuck to my forehead and pull my knees up to my chest. I grasp around in my head for other things to think about. Nachos or bird place mats or the Pythagorean theorem. It doesn't work. I picture our muddy fairy-tale dresses. Daniella and I were magical once. But now our potions are drained, our capes torn, our crowns snapped in two.

Everything is cursed.

15

The Citadel

I'm in the middle of the first Math Olympics assessment, and I can't stop thinking about seaweed-covered gowns. About the last entry I read in Daniella's diary—how badly she wanted to grow up, until she actually did.

I wish we could go back to the way things were. Like on our trip to Puerto Rico, when we drove from Titi Celina's to Old San Juan and visited the citadel at El Morro with Buelo and Buela.

"What do you think?" Buelo asked me. He didn't need a wheelchair or a cane.

"It's amazing," I said. The hills around the citadel matched his accent. Soft and rolling.

Someone flew a red kite in the middle of the grass. I tracked its string all the way up, to where the kite pressed into the sky. I didn't know anything could be that blue.

There were almost a hundred stairs in the citadel. Daniella and I walked down them, and Buela and Buelo stayed on a bench in the shade. We were covered in sweat by the time we reached the bottom. The stairs ended on a big stone ledge, with old rusted cannons at the edges and a black gate surrounding the whole thing. I imagined hiding in this fort while a war broke out beyond the walls.

"Over here, Cass," Daniella called to me from the gate. I stood next to her, looking out at the shimmering sea. It stretched out toward tree-covered islands in the distance.

"It's so pretty," I said. But it was more than that. Everything was perfect. The kite against the clouds, the water, Daniella's shoulder leaning into mine.

I draw hills and stone buildings and stairs on my assessment, memories where I still believed I was good enough. But I forget how to feel that way now. I can only focus on the words in Daniella's diary, and the things she said at Kindly Vines. My scarecrow hair. Daniella was the one to find me drenching my hair in gel that night after Communion class.

"What are you doing? Your hair is supposed to be wet when you use this," she said, taking the purple bottle out of my hand.

"They couldn't tell I was Puerto Rican," I said.

"Who?"

"The girls in my class. They said I looked like a scarecrow."

Daniella put the gel bottle back in its place under the sink.

"Those girls wish their hair was as nice as yours. It's as fierce as a lion's mane. The Puerto Rican part of you is there even if you can't see it." She turned the faucet on full blast and told me to put my head under the water. Her fingers *worked through the hardened knots I'd made, until they loosened.*

I erase my drawings so hard that the paper rips.

"Ten minutes left," Mr. G says.

There are five questions on the assessment. I've finished zero. I look around. Sage's pencil moves quickly over the paper, her face scrunched up in concentration. Emilio counts something off with his fingers. Aaron taps on his desk. I try to read the first question again.

-3+(-3)-3+(-3)-3

I stare at the threes until they look like eights and hearts and fish. I forget if the sum of a bunch of negatives is eventually positive, or if it just stays negative forever.

"Time's up. Place your papers facedown on my desk on your way out. And try not to pat yourselves on the back *too* hard. I need you all uninjured for Regionals."

The only line filled out on my assessment is my name. I don't want to turn it in. I'm supposed to be good at math, but nothing is like it's supposed to be anymore. Mr. G smiles when I drop my assessment onto his desk. I rush out the door.

"Wait up." Aaron's voice echoes behind me in the hall. I look over my shoulder.

"What?" It comes out sharp. His face looks like I've stabbed him. I keep walking. He catches up to me easily with his long legs.

"That was pretty tough," he says. I don't know if he

means the assessment or the way I snapped at him.

I'm tired of trying to solve problems. We've reached the front doors now. I see Mom's minivan through a space between two buses, parked in a spot by a huge oak tree. Ben and Jac are already out by the car. We're doing homework at my house tonight.

Aaron wraps the straps of his backpack around his wrists. They look like twisted green vines in a garden. I think about Aaron's North Sapling story, his Monopoly shoe buried under the dirt. The story distracted me from the mess inside my head.

I need more distraction.

"Do you want to come over?" I ask.

His face loses its wounded look. He drops his backpack straps.

"Sure. I'll tell you about Elmtown." We walk through that space between the buses, even though we're not supposed to. The monitors always tell us we can get crushed as flat as a pancake.

"You'll have a bigger audience," I say. Jac spins Ben in place by the minivan. She stops when she sees us.

"Who are you?" Jac asks when we reach them.

"Aaron. We have three classes together," Aaron says.

"What are you doing *here*, Aaron of three of my classes?"

"I heard we're visiting Cassi's estate, Jac of the blue-haired."

Jac squints. Her hair is still as blue as it was the day we made nachos. I can only imagine the fights she and Uncle Eric are having about it when we're not around.

"Great. Now there's two of them," Ben says. He stumbles a little from the spinning but manages to open the minivan door. We all climb in. Mom watches us in the rearview mirror. Aaron sticks his hand out to her.

"I'm Aaron Kale."

Mom shakes his hand.

"He's in Math Olympics with me," I tell her.

"Very nice. Do you have permission to come over, Aaron?"

"My dad lets me do anything that might lead to a story."

I think twelve years of minivan rides with Jac has taught Mom to handle responses like that. She nods, adjusts her mirrors, and pulls out of the spot.

"Your last name is a vegetable," Jac whispers into Aaron's ear.

"Your name rhymes with 'snack,'" he whispers back.

Jac leans into her seat.

"He can stay," she says.

16

Elmtown

Buela is in the kitchen when we get home. She has her own key to our house. I joke with her about how she's breaking in, but I actually love when she shows up unannounced. A pot bubbles on the stove. There's a plate of sliced, flattened plantains on the counter.

"Buela's making tostones!" Jac announces. She says it like "toe stones." I imagine having rocks where my feet should be.

"Tosto-*nes*. Like '*Yes*, more tosto-*nes*.'" Buela used little memory devices like that when she was teaching me Spanish. She pats Jac on the head with a spoon. She isn't Jac's grandma, but Jac calls her "Buela" anyway. So does Ben.

"What are tostones?" Aaron asks.

"Fried plantains," I tell him. "They're like chips but a thousand times better."

Buela crosses the kitchen. She stops in front of Aaron and puts her arms up. He's at least a foot and a half taller than my tiny Buela.

"Come, come." She waves her hands. Aaron bends

down to hug her like this isn't the first time they've met. It makes me feel warm. I take off my jacket.

"Where's Dani?" Jac looks around the kitchen like Daniella might be hiding behind the fridge or under the floor tiles.

Buela shrugs. "*No se.* I walk in, she walks out. Barely a hello." She drops a plantain into the hot oil. It sizzles like a loud burst of static.

I watch the plantain sink to the bottom of the pot.

"Sorry, Buela. Dad says she's just adjusting," I say.

Aaron looks like he might ask a thousand questions that I don't want to answer. *Who is Daniella? What is she adjusting to?*

"Oh, I know. It's not so long ago I was a teenager too." Buela stirs the oil with her slotted spoon and smiles at me. I wrap my arms around her shoulders. She pats my hand until I'm ready to let go.

Jac, Ben, and Aaron are already assembled at the kitchen table when I come over, textbooks and binders spread out in front of them. Aaron is in the spot next to me, at the hummingbird place mat.

"Do we have to do homework, or can we just pretend? Because the next episode is about a haunted movie theater." Jac pulls out her phone. I happen to know she has the documentary series loaded on there.

"We have to do work." I'm so not in the mood for ghosts. Then again, is anyone ever in the mood for ghosts?

Do people wake up in the morning and think, *Hey, I really feel like being haunted today?*

"Don't be a baby, Cassandra."

"Don't be a bully, Jaclyn."

She smiles at me. It's scarier than all the episodes of the documentary series put together.

"First, I have a deal to fulfill with Cassi," Aaron says. "I'm supposed to tell her about Elmtown, Texas."

"Like from the country song?" Ben asks.

"Yeah, actually."

Ben stands up. *"I'll meet you out in Elmtown. Say you won't let me down."* He sings into an open yellow highlighter like it's a microphone. Aaron looks both surprised and impressed at his outburst.

"Pitchy," Jac says. Ben swipes the highlighter across Jac's arm. It leaves a line like the tail of a shooting star.

"Elmtown is only known for two things. That song and the mountains," Aaron says.

Jac puts her phone back on the table. I almost sigh with relief. Aaron clears his throat.

"It was the mountains that made Dad want to move there. He said there were lots of metaphors at the top. So we set out to climb one on a foggy day in April. He said we'd have to take the most challenging path. That it wouldn't be much of a story if we didn't—"

"*Ahem,*" Jac interrupts. "If we're telling campfire stories, I'll need to grab a flashlight. Also, we'll need fire."

Jac rubs two pencils together so hard, they might actually spark. I pull them out of her hands.

"Shh. I want to hear about Elmtown," Ben says. He leans onto his elbows.

My best friends + my deal with Aaron = A giddiness inside me that makes my teeth chatter.

"Dad said every obstacle was an opportunity for growth. He'd say that whenever we had to climb over a tree branch or an especially knobby root. I think he would've been glad if we ran into a bear, just for the sake of having an obstacle. Eventually we made it to the top."

Buela takes that moment to walk over with the finished tostones. She puts a towel on the table and the plate on top. The yellow discs shine with salt.

"You are a wonderful storyteller. Like my husband," Buela says. She sits down with us. "May I stay for the rest?"

Aaron nods and takes a breath.

"We were alone up there. I walked as close as I could to the edge and looked down. If I'd fallen, I would've slipped through miles of pine trees. It was cold out but the sun was warm, and I started to wonder if anything could convince a person more that everything would be okay."

Aaron looks at the hummingbird place mat. His cheeks turn red, maybe from the heat wafting off the tostones.

"'I can't do it,' I heard Dad say. I turned around. He was sitting on a rock with his shoulders slumped, glasses in his hand. I asked him what he meant. 'I can't describe it,' he continued. He said he couldn't put meaning into any of it."

I hear Buela sniffle. She has her hands clutched to her heart. Jac stuffs two tostones into her mouth but doesn't say a word.

"So I said, 'We're here together. Isn't that all the meaning we need? Isn't that enough?' Then he put his glasses back on like he needed to see me better to say whatever he was going to say. And he said, 'Sure, Aaron. Sure, that's enough.'"

Jac's chewing and Buela's sniffles are the only sounds in the kitchen.

"Then what?" I ask in a quiet voice.

"That's it. That's how the memoir chapter 'Enough' came to be. I think it's one of the best. Can I try those?" Aaron points to the plate of tostones. Buela holds them out to him like a gift.

"Beautiful story," she says when he takes one.

"Even better than the song," Ben says. He starts singing the chorus again.

I think about Aaron at the top of a mountain with his dad, about Daniella and me on the ledge at that citadel. Moments like that always feel so big and important. But maybe sitting at the kitchen table with bird place mats is big and important too, as long as we're together.

"These are incredible," Aaron says to Buela. She beams.

I add *likes Buela's incredible food* to my set of Aaron Facts.

17

Oral Hygiene

I share a bathroom with Daniella. We redecorated it together two summers ago. It took us an hour to figure out how to use the plastic hooks to hang the butterfly shower curtain. I'm still not sure we did it right. In the basement Daniella found framed pictures of a beach in Puerto Rico. She tacked them to the bathroom walls.

"Butterfly beach. That's a theme, right?" she asked.

I hung two yellow towels on a bronze bar. One for each of us.

"Of course."

I'm at the sink brushing my teeth when Daniella walks in. Her pajama pants have turtles on them.

"Sorry. Didn't know you were in here," she says.

Her presence gives me an idea. I brush my teeth extra hard for a second so that the toothpaste bubbles in my mouth. I lean my head back a little.

"Ishh okay. Cawhm in," I gurgle.

Daniella rolls her eyes. It's not the reaction I wanted, but she does come in and takes her toothbrush from the left wing of the butterfly holder.

Oral Hygiene

We used to have gurgled conversations while we brushed our teeth, our mouths full of spit and foam.

"Youwah loo ridiculoush," Daniella said.

"Wha?" I answered, my eyes watering from laughter and the taste of spearmint.

"Youwah loo ridiculoush!"

"So oo youwah!"

Mom passed by in the hall with a laundry basket.

"You are compromising your oral hygiene."

"Showwy, Mawm," we said, and kept brushing, eyes still laughing and locked on each other in the mirror.

Daniella brushes with one arm crossed over her stomach, her eyes on the ceiling. She doesn't try to speak, just spits every once in a while. All my teeth feel pretty brushed now. I start to taste blood. But I keep going anyway, waiting and hoping for Daniella to catch my eye in the mirror and call me ridiculous.

October 5

Want to hear some bad combinations?

Six a.m. alarms and not being able to sleep.

Jenna talking about the homecoming dance
and me not even wanting to go.

Friends and fake smiles.

Being near my family and reminding myself
how I've let them all down.

I want to be the person I used to be for them.
For Cassi, Jac, Ben.

They were always there. For random
midnights, lazy Sundays, Chinese food in front
of the TV. Holiday get-togethers and small,
meaningless moments. The years where it was
okay to pretend to be things we weren't.

They were a different kind of friends to me
than Jenna or anyone at school. We were part of
each other.

In the back of my mind, I've always realized
that I'm older. That they looked up to me. They
depended on me to do the scary things first, like

change in the locker room for gym class or fall in love. It was up to me to report back and say, "There's nothing to be afraid of."

But I can't be that person for them right now. Maybe not ever again. So it's better to just stay away.

18

Piñata

The cafeteria puts out a calendar every month that lists the daily hot lunches. The October calendar is orange, and the *O* is a pumpkin. Pretty much every square has the words "fruit cup" and "milk" in it, except for Monday, October 8. That box just says *Fiesta Day*.

The smell of spicy peppers and packaged seasoned meat hits me halfway down the hall. I look around. The cafeteria is decorated in all different Hispanic cultures. A banner that says FIESTA and a piñata hang from the ceiling. Miniature sombreros sit in neat rows on the tables. Jac and I get into the hot-lunch line.

I see rice and pinto beans, beef in a deep red sauce. It looks like Buela's food, but something isn't quite right. The rice isn't yellow enough. The meat seems spongy. The food is like me—it doesn't look the way it's supposed to. I walk past the prepared trays without grabbing one.

"Aren't you going to get something?" Jac asks.

"Not hungry."

A wire is strung above the register, with the flags of

Spanish-speaking places attached. The Puerto Rican one is in the middle. Jac perches a miniature sombrero on her head when we sit down next to each other. It's a burnt berry color, like her hair.

"Why is your hair still blue, Jac?" I ask. I pick up a few strands and rub them between my fingers, like that might reveal the truth. The strands stay quiet and dark.

She spears a pinto bean.

"You really want to know?" she asks.

"Now I'm nervous, but yes."

Jac grins. The green beans on her tray shrivel up even more than they already were.

"I've been dying it over and over again."

"Jac!" I don't know what I was expecting. Of course she has been. "You're going to get in so much trouble. Stop doing that."

She ignores me and picks up her plastic knife.

"I'm serious, Jac. Promise you'll stop?" I demand.

If Uncle Eric finds out, she'll be grounded for life. When we all got in trouble for writing on Jac's wall, we weren't allowed to see each other for a week. The Chordays are already down one member. We can't lose Jac, too.

"Okay, okay, I promise. Do you want my Leslies?" Jac asks. She points with the plastic knife to her green beans, made "Spanish" by mixing them with salsa. Apparently Jac despises Leslies as much as she does most vegetables. I think about the bad combinations Daniella wrote down in her diary. Green beans and salsa should be included on the list.

Before I can answer, Ben and Aaron walk over with their own hot lunch trays and sit across from us. Aaron takes the spot in front of me. He started sitting at our table the day after he told us about Elmtown.

"Did you see it?" Ben asks.

"See what?" Jac scoops up a few of her "Leslies" and puts them on Ben's tray. He hunches over his tray so she can't do it again.

"The video," Aaron answers for him.

I look around the cafeteria and see lots of bowed heads, the classic sign of looking at a forbidden cell phone.

"I haven't seen anything," I say.

"Here." I feel something nudge my knee. I look down and see Aaron's phone outstretched. Our fingers brush accidentally when I take it, which for some reason feels like I'm being shocked. I add *electric fingers* to my set of Aaron Facts, and then hold the phone between Jac and me.

She presses play on the video. I see the Eliza T. Dakota cafeteria, a table like the one we're sitting at now. The camera shifts to the end of the table, where an eighth-grade boy and girl are standing, facing each other. They're yelling, but I can't hear for sure what they're saying. I think the girl's mouth forms "How could you." Then she picks up a scoop of the same rice we're eating now and throws it at him.

"Oof," Jac says. *"No bueno."*

I click off the phone and put it next to Aaron's tray, so there won't be any accidental contact this time. He slides it quickly off the table and into his lap.

"Get it?" Jac asks. *"No bueno.* 'Cause it's fiesta day."

"I get it," I say.

A group at a table nearby starts to laugh. Someone shouts, "Ooh, she got him!" I've seen that same couple walk down the hall with their arms linked. The boy was in my Metals class last year and stamped the girl's name into the hooks he made.

What was going on that no one could see?

One of the lunch monitors clears his throat into a microphone. "We're going to start the piñata." He holds a wooden stick in his hand. "Line up if you want a go."

I stand up.

"You're trying it?" Jac asks.

"Yeah, why not?"

The lunch monitor wraps a bandana around my head when it's my turn. Everything goes black. I regret getting in line, start to panic at the idea of swinging out of control.

"Three tries. Good luck." He puts the wooden stick in my hand.

I step forward and swing. The stick slices through

the air without making contact. I steady myself, adjusting to the blindness. My next try grazes what might be the edge of the piñata. Maybe the donkey's confetti tail. I swing again as hard as I can, feel the wooden stick dig into the cardboard body, hear the candy rain to the ground. A swarm has already attacked the stash by the time I pull my blindfold off, including Jac. The little sombrero hangs off the back of her neck by its string.

"Go grab some. You broke it," the lunch monitor says.

He nudges me toward the chaos, but my feet don't move. The piñata lies on its side, bleeding sugar-free lollipops and fruit snacks all over the floor, its mouth a little bit open like it wants to ask me, *How could you?*

19

Tangles

My hair likes to tie itself up. I know everyone's hair does that and that's why conditioner exists, but mine is so thick that the knots form in deep, hard-to reach places. Splitting it into sections helps, but even then I still miss spots.

I stand in front of my mirror and brush. The bristles make a horrible sound when they rip through. In the reflection, I can see my door open wider. Mom steps in.

"That sounds like it hurts," she says.

It does.

"Uncle Eric is going to make Jac cut her hair off if the blue doesn't come out. Maybe I should do the same thing," I say.

Mom comes over.

"You got this hair from me. As thick as anything." She takes the brush and gathers up a chunk of my hair. She works the bristles through the knot. It pulls, but not as much. "Still very beautiful."

I look at Mom in the mirror. She has dark, glossy hair, cut short to her ears. I've seen it long only in pictures.

"Your hair was like this too?"

"I'm sure I've told you that. Your Buela had to brush it for me all the time."

I imagine Mom standing with Buela in front a mirror like this one, experiencing that same tug from a painful knot. Did she ever feel the way I've been feeling lately? That everything was changing too fast?

"I guess I forgot."

Earlier today when we went to see Buelo, Mom tucked a white blanket up under his chin. Her face looked like she was remembering something, maybe being twelve like me, walking with Buelo through the zoo in Mayagüez. Mom said they lived close enough that sometimes she could hear the lions roaring from her backyard.

She keeps brushing. Soon the bristles glide through the strands without catching on anything. Mom puts the brush on my dresser. Her other hand rests on my arm.

"*Todo estara bien,*" she says. I can't tell whether it's the look in my eyes or the knots in my hair that make her say that.

"Are you sure?" I ask.

"Yes." She kisses the top of my head. "I'm sure."

For a second I feel less tangled.

"Thanks, Mom."

She walks out of my room and leaves the door a few

inches more cracked than it was before. I run my hand through my hair. It might shoot out sharply sometimes, and it's not dark and shiny, but it's still thick like my mom's. The thought makes me smile.

Lesson Four of Math Olympics: Equality means that two things are mathematically the same. Even if I'm 4+1 and you're 2+3, we both still equal 5. It's that simple.

20

Extra Time

Daniella and I used to take the bus together. Now she leaves twenty-five minutes before me. Every morning I wake up earlier than I have to, so we can still have our breakfasts together at the kitchen table.

Today she sits at the toucan place mat with a bowl of Lucky Charms. Daniella only eats the marshmallows, which I think is madness, since the plain pieces are equally as good, but at least it's something about her I can still recognize.

"What are you wearing to the dance?" I ask her.

"How did you know about that?" She talks through a mouthful of cereal.

I panic.

Daniella x Finding out I read her diary = Breakfast alone from now on.

"Ben's tap class is at the high school this session. He saw a flyer."

"Oh. Well, I don't know yet." She takes one last bite of Lucky Charms and then puts her backpack on. I wonder what's inside. Maybe *The Chemical Property of*

Life. Through our living room windows, I see her bus drive up. It slows to a stop at the end of our driveway. Daniella heads for the door.

"You're going to look beautiful," I say to her back. Her curls are pulled up into a messy bun.

"Thanks, Cass." Her voice gets caught in the closing door.

I dump my own cereal bowl into the sink. All that's left of our sister breakfast are soggy rainbows and the sound of a school bus pulling away.

21

Be Better

I fill up my water bottle in the wing near the shop classes, the fountain closest to study hall. Daniella bought the water bottle for me at the education store in the mall. It's green with the words "Eat. Math. Repeat." on it.

"Can we talk for a second, Cassi?" a voice asks from behind me. I turn and see Mr. G. His face looks serious. I wish he'd make a joke or do a bad impression, but he doesn't.

"Okay." I forget that I'm filling up a water bottle. It spills over and my hand gets all wet.

The sound of hammering carries down the hall. When I took Metals last year, I liked it a hundred times more than I thought I would. Maybe because there was so much math involved. I helped everyone in class convert their measurements. Except for Jac, who wanted the legs on the table she made to be uneven. She got a C+. I still use my table for the little figurines Titi Celina sends me. I have a frog and a cactus and a mermaid holding a pearl.

"I don't want you to think I'm disappointed when I

say this," Mr. G says. But he wouldn't say that unless I've done something disappointing. "I had to count up the answers on the assessments to send in to the Math Olympics peeps, and I noticed you didn't do yours."

"I'm sorry," I say. I stare at the floor.

"There's no need to apologize. I don't want you to be any better than your best, Cassi. But I know that wasn't it."

A drill starts buzzing in the Metals room.

"What if it was?"

What if I'm not that good at math? What if it just seemed like I was because I can add things up fast and convert millimeters into inches in Metals class?

"Hey there. That's a personal foul." Mr. G karate chops the air like a referee. It makes me look up. A smile tugs at my cheeks. "Unnecessary roughness. Fifteen-yard penalty."

Mr. G waves his hands like he's shooing me. I start to back away. My ballet flats squeak on the linoleum floor.

"Stop!" I've traveled the assigned fifteen yards and end up next to the Metals workshop. I look inside. A new set of students is working on their tables. I want to tell them how it felt to put something together with my own hands, piece by piece. That there are 25.4 millimeters in an inch. Mr. G whistles through his fingers.

"I believe in you, Cassi," he shouts down the hall.

The signal to switch classes goes off, and a crowd forms between us. Mr. G gives me two thumbs-up above everyone's heads.

It's completely embarrassing and exactly what I needed.

22

Juniper

The second Math Olympics assessment goes much different from the first. I keep my mind on the numbers, where it's supposed to be. *Lesson Seven of Math Olympics* is written on the board—*Focus, focus, focus.* There's not a single doodle on my paper when I finish.

Mr. G gives me a look when I put my assessment on his desk. His eyes seem to ask, *How did it go?* I try to nod back in a way that says, *Great* and *Thanks for everything* at the same time. My phone buzzes in my back pocket when I get into the hall. I read the message from Mom.

Running late. Library meeting. Be there soon.

I find an empty bench outside and think about Buelo. He'd like to be sitting out here, even if the wind is cold. I hope we go to see him soon. I hope we can sit together outside on the patio at Kindly Vines when the weather gets warm, away from the smell of sickness and the get-well balloons.

"It's like Juniper, Maine, out here."

I look up, and Aaron is there. He sits on the bench

next to me. His legs stretch out so much farther than mine. "It gets below zero all the time. It's the only tree town I got to pick."

"Why did you choose somewhere so cold?" I ask.

"They have the largest aviation museum in New England."

I settle in for another story.

"Planes are cool but don't seem worth the frostbite," I say.

Aaron laughs.

"They were worth it in fifth grade. I made models and everything. When my class took a field trip to the museum and Dad volunteered to chaperone, I didn't even care that he brought his notebook with him. Because I was going to see what put planes up in the sky."

Wind cuts him off. It grazes my cheeks like shards of ice. We burrow deeper into our jackets.

"There was this one display of the inside of a cockpit. It looked like an interactive display, one where you could go in and press the buttons and stuff, but there was a velvet rope around the whole thing with a sign that said DO NOT TOUCH."

"Did you steal a plane, Aaron?" My voice is muffled by my collar.

Aaron doesn't laugh this time. His face is bright pink with cold.

"Dad started to step over the rope. The kids in my

group were laughing, but it made me nervous. You're not supposed to cross those ropes. It's pretty much the number one rule of museums. He climbed up the display and sat right in the pilot's seat. He moved one of the levers, and it popped off in his hand."

Aaron fidgets with the zipper on his jacket. "Dad still had that lever in his hand when the security guard caught him. He got kicked out. He couldn't be in the building for the rest of the trip, so my group got absorbed into the other ones. It was hard to focus on the planes after that."

The late buses start hissing, signaling the last call to get on.

"My dad ran a red light once," I say, even though it's nothing compared to what Aaron just told me. At least it makes him smile a little. He has a dimple in his cheek.

Aaron stands up from the bench. "That was the first time I realized that my whole life had become Dad making decisions and me having to deal with the consequences, even if it seemed fun at first."

"That's kind of a sad story," I say.

Aaron shrugs. "Some stories are like that."

I think about what Daniella used to say about sad songs. That they can make you feel understood. Maybe that theory can apply to stories, too.

"Why couldn't your mom stop him from dragging you around?" I ask.

The color drains from Aaron's face. The first bus in the line starts to drive off.

"Shoot. I have to go." He runs all the way to Bus 39.

I might have to add a set of Aaron Secrets.

23

Homecoming

Daniella wears a red dress to homecoming. Mom tied a French braid in the front of Daniella's hair and pinned it back into her curls with a sparkly clip. I'm sitting on the couch, eyes fixed on the shiny streaks of bronzer on Daniella's cheeks. Dad is in one of the recliners watching a football game. Daniella stares out the front window, waiting for the flash of Jenna's mom's headlights.

"Your first high school dance," Mom murmurs. She lifts her camera and takes a picture of Daniella pulling the curtain back.

"It's not a big deal," she says. She sits next to me. Her dress poofs up around her.

"Are you sure Jenna can't come in to take pictures?" Mom asks.

"We're already running late. We'll take some there, I promise."

Mom frowns but doesn't push further; there's a line drawn in the carpet that she can't cross.

"At least take one with your sister," she says. She

makes a clapping motion, telling us to move in. Daniella sighs under her breath.

"Come here, Cass," she says, and wraps her bare arm around my shoulders.

Does she know how many days it's been since we sat like this? Because I've lost count. I smell her coconut-mint body spray.

Mom snaps the picture. I try to see us like the camera lens does. A girl with bronze cheeks and a red dress on her way to a high school homecoming. Another girl with dull hair and sweatpants, who stood in a corner during the Welcome to Middle School dance. Would the camera even guess we were sisters?

The window lights up and a car horn beeps outside. Daniella lets me go. She slips her sandals on by the door. They're shiny and black with a little cork-colored wedge heel. I have the same pair. We bought them in one of the shops in San Juan, and then kept walking, arms linked, down the cobblestone streets, the plastic bags bumping against our legs.

"Have fun," Dad says, and stands up from the recliner, like he couldn't bear to look at her until the last minute. His eyes are glossy when he hugs her. "My high schooler."

Daniella steps out onto the front porch and waves good-bye.

"I want to hear everything!" I call after her.

The door closes before I can tell if she heard me.

October 21

I've noticed that my feelings aren't a constant
thing. There are seconds when I almost feel
better. I'll get super interested in a reading
Ms. Murphy assigns for American Studies, or
randomly excited about the ugly-sweater party
Jenna is planning for December.

I think about inviting Cass into my room and
being a real older sister again. I could tell her
about how bad the music was at homecoming
last night, but that it didn't matter because
everyone sang along anyway.

Those are good seconds.

And then a thousand-pound weight crashes
down on my head, and I remember.

I remember that Buelo lives at Kindly Vines.
I remember the way his face contorted when we
moved him in. I know Buela and Mom feel bad
that I was there that day. We visited him last
week, and Buela handed me a bundle of smiley-
face balloons to carry down the hall.

"To cheer you up. And the room," she said.

I wanted to pop every one of those balloons. When Buelo started to get mad later, Mom whisked me into the hall, sent me on a pointless errand to get her sudoku book out of the car.

But they can't take back what I saw.

Sometimes I look in the mirror, and it's Buelo staring back at me. We've always had things in common. A flair for the historical. A love for sugary cereal.

And now, the forgetting. Him forgetting who he is and me forgetting how to stay happy.

24

An Unexpected Snowstorm

The first week of November brings an unexpected snowstorm, though "storm" might be an exaggeration. It's more of a powdered-sugar-on-fried-dough dusting. The school declares an early dismissal anyway. I call Mom from the office to get permission to go to Jac's. Aaron comes too.

Jac and I pull on fleece leggings under sweatpants and wrap ourselves in scarves. Aaron puts on two pairs of Uncle Eric's flannel pajama pants that Jac stole out of the dryer. Aaron's tall enough to fit in them. Jac calls up the stairs to tell Uncle Eric that we'll be sledding on the hill. All we hear back is heavy metal, the music he listens to while doing the Holy Baloney payroll. Ben is at the hill already when we get there, wearing a bright red snowsuit with straps that look like velvet. A saucer-shaped sled rests at his feet.

"Don't you dare," he warns.

"Don't I dare what?" Jac asks, her voice all sweet and innocent.

"You know what."

"Talk about your transformation into a marsh-mallow?"

"I'll be warmer than you." He sticks out his hip, then presses a finger to his padded side and makes a sizzling sound.

I laugh out loud. An icy breeze slips through my scarf, but I can feel the sun, too. I think about Aaron's mountain story.

"You were right," I tell him.

He looks at me. "Of course I was. About what?"

The blend of cold and sunshine. I do feel like everything is going to be okay.

I get choked up. Sometimes the words in my head feel too big to say out loud.

"Never mind." I hand him a sled. It's round with one dip in the edge, like a doughnut with a bite taken out.

A layer of snow glitters across the hill—ideal sledding conditions. The thin, wet stuff is the most slippery. We get settled onto our sleds. Jac takes the big square that looks like an oversize lunch tray, and I get the long, narrow one that two people can fit on.

"Ready . . . set . . ." Jac takes off before saying "go," but the rest of us are right behind her.

The wind blows my scarf around. Jac is still ahead, and Ben and Aaron fall behind. I lean forward to gain speed, but the sled was made for two people. The empty back lifts up, and the front end grinds into the snow. It slows me down. Ben beats me to the bottom of the hill. Aaron and I slide through the finish line at the same time.

"First place goes to the Dark Lord, second to Marshmallow Man, and last place to the Mathletes," Jac announces.

I don't care that I lost the race. I'm thinking about when Daniella used to sit in the back of the sled.

This sled – Daniella = A hunk of plastic that doesn't function properly.

We start to climb back to the starting point. Aaron dumps his bitten doughnut into the snow.

"I'll go down with you," he says once we're at the top, and sits in the two-person sled, filling up the empty space behind me.

His knees brush up against my back. He grips the side of the sled with pale white hands.

"Here we go." I tip forward, and we take off, sliding faster and faster, with Jac and Ben behind us. I watch Aaron hold on tighter. We reach the bottom before I can think too hard about why his hands make my stomach flip over.

Jac gets off her sled and stares up the hill. Her eyes are gray and stormy. Blue hair whips around her face, darker than ever. It must be the shadows from the trees; she promised me she would stop dying it.

"Mind if we join?"

Uncle Eric and Leslie are at the top of the hill. She wears a skirt with black stockings and Uncle Eric's Patriots jacket, which doesn't seem like a great choice for sledding.

"Yes, we mind," Jac calls to them. "Please return to your payroll."

The wind blows harder, like a natural disaster is on its way.

"That's not how this works, Jac," Uncle Eric says.

Leslie rubs her arms. Jac starts to walk. She retraces our footsteps all the way to her back door. Ben and Aaron and I follow.

"Sorry, Uncle Eric," I say when I pass. He touches my arm with his gloved hand.

"She'll come around." I don't know if he's saying it to Leslie or to me.

I leave the two-person sled by Jac's back steps, and then go inside. The rush of warmth thaws my cheeks. Jac's footsteps stomp around in her room upstairs.

"Should we go after her?" I ask.

"She'll probably throw things," Ben says.

"Are we talking rocks or pillows?" Aaron asks. Ben and I look at him. He nods like he understands—it could be anything. We head up the stairs.

I knock on Jac's door.

"Don't come in here. Seriously," Jac says. I twist the knob. It doesn't budge.

"Jac, unlock the door," I say.

"No. Go to Ben's. I'll meet you there."

I elbow Ben. "Get it."

Ben lifts the little gnome outside Uncle Eric's office and grabs the bobby pin hidden underneath. He hands it to me. I straighten it out and then stick the wavy metal into the hole in the center of the doorknob. Aaron watches Operation Jac with wide eyes.

"And don't you use a . . ." We bust through Jac's door. "Pin."

We stare each other down—the three of us at the door, Jac at her mirror. She stirs a giant bowl of blue Kool-Aid.

"What are you doing?" I ask.

"I thought I'd found all your pins." She drops the wooden spoon into the liquid.

Ben steps closer to her setup. "Have you been dying your hair this whole time?" His voice is slow and cautious.

Jac lifts her chin. "Yes."

I follow Ben. Ripped packets of Kool-Aid spill out on Jac's dresser—two blue raspberries, a black cherry, and a grape.

"You promised, Jac," I snap. I don't feel like being slow and cautious.

"Promised what?" Ben asks.

"That she'd stop. But I guess she likes making Uncle Eric mad too much to care about that."

Jac picks up a rubber glove and throws it at my head. "You don't know anything about it!" she says.

The blue liquid trembles in its bowl. Jac goes to sit on her bed. She wears an Eliza T. Dakota T-shirt from the school store. The shoulders are covered in blue spots. Ben and I sit on either side of her. Aaron stands near the dyeing site on her dresser like maybe he shouldn't be here. But I can't picture this moment without him in it. He's now a factor in this equation.

"Tell us, then," Ben says.

Jac stares at her camouflage comforter.

"If Dad's mad at me, he won't pay attention to *her*," she mumbles.

Guilt creeps in because of the way I yelled. *Lesson Nine of Math Olympics: Sometimes numbers can be irrational. But let's not love them any less.*

"It doesn't really seem to be . . . working, though," I say gently.

Her chin wobbles.

"I'm aware, Cassi. He's like a stupid lovesick teenager. I don't want to fight with him about it anymore. But I can't stop. As long as we're fighting, it means he still knows I exist. I have power over that."

I wrap my arms around Jac, my head pressed against hers. Ben shakes his shoulders and leans into her side.

"He's never going to forget about you," I say. "You're his world."

"His whole, infuriating world," Ben adds.

Jac leans into me. She smells like the artificial blue raspberries.

"My mom loved birds," Aaron says from the dresser. We all look up.

"To quote Mrs. Quan's comment on my last essay: 'Please try to stay on topic,'" Jac says.

"It reminded me of what you said about having power. I thought if I could build enough birdhouses, my mom would never leave. I made so many. She would smear the perches with peanut butter and seeds, and soon we had a whole neighborhood of singing things." Aaron swirls his fingers in the bowl of Kool-Aid like he's trying to make a wave pool. "But she still left."

I imagine the place mats on my kitchen table coming to life and living in Aaron's birdhouse village.

"Your mom left you?" I ask.

Aaron nods. "I guess what she loved most about birds is that they could take off."

It's quiet except for the Kool-Aid sloshing up against the sides of the bowl.

Ben stands from the bed and walks over to Aaron. His snow pants make a *swish* sound. He reaches up to his head and lifts something invisible, and then puts it on Aaron.

"You are officially the Monologue King." Ben bows. "All hail."

"All hail," Jac and I repeat. Aaron tries to look humble, but a smile splits his face. I add to my set of Aaron Facts. *Has a mom who left. He tried to get her to stay. Monologue King.*

"Which tree town was that in?" I ask.

"This was before the tree towns. It just . . ." He wipes the Kool-Aid from his fingers off on Uncle Eric's flannel pants. "Seemed like something you would tell a friend to show them they're not alone." He glances at Jac.

She smiles back. A lightbulb flickers in the ceiling fan.

"We're not friends," Jac says. Aaron's expression looks like he understands her dark humor already. I realize that he wasn't just a factor here. In this moment, he was the solution.

Jac bursts away. She reaches for the Kool-Aid packets and squeeze bottles and tosses them at all of us like she's not going to need them anymore.

25

Family Night

Kindly Vines hosts a potluck dinner in the middle of November. They call it Family Night. We pick Buela up from the condo. It's five o'clock but pitch-black outside. I think that's the worst part of winter approaching. How there's still plenty of day left but it feels like the middle of the night.

Buela gets in on my side. We're driving Dad's car instead of the minivan, so I have to squeeze in between her and Daniella.

"You want to hold this?" Buela puts an insulated food carrier in my lap before I answer; she knows I like to hold her trays. It warms me more than the heat blasting out of the car's vents. I take a breath. She definitely made arroz con gandules.

I lean the tray a little toward Daniella. She loves Buela's rice and peas. I hope its powers might break whatever sad spell she's under. She's been especially silent tonight. Her head leans against the window. Orange streetlights streak across her face while Dad drives.

"Keep it straight," Buela says.

I hold the tray flat again.

The drive to Kindly Vines takes twenty minutes. We file out of the car when Dad parks in the lot. The walls at the reception area are painted a color between white and purple. Something about it makes me dizzy. We're signing in when a nurse comes over.

"You're Mr. Francesca's family, correct?" she asks.

Her eyes are wide and frantic. A chill slips down my spine.

"We are," Mom says. She squeezes the sign-in pen. It's attached to the clipboard by a white string. I think about the kite I saw at El Morro, stretched up into the sky.

"Places like this are made for flying, sí?" Buelo asked when he caught me staring.

Kindly Vines is not a place made for flying.

"We're having a bit of a rough time getting him to the potluck. Maybe you can come turn him around?"

Mom nods. Dad holds her hand while we walk, quickly, to room 201. Buela holds on to my arm.

I hear Buelo before I see him.

"No, no, no. You cannot make me." Bits of Spanish and swear words mix in. Buela lets go and jogs into Buelo's room as fast as her short legs can take her. The tray of rice and peas shakes in my hands.

"Wait outside," Dad says to Daniella and me. My parents follow Buela. Daniella and I stop near the bathroom, just before Buelo's room, where Daniella's words are still shouting at me. I can hear them, as loud as the words coming from Buelo's room.

"Calmate, mi amor, calmate," Buela urges.

I try to calm down like Buela is asking Buelo to do.

"Why am I here? Why am I here?" Buelo's voice begins to strain. I could sink under the weight of these rice and peas. Daniella leans against the wall and covers her face with her hand.

Down the hall, people stare. They hold their own trays of food for the potluck and push their own parents and grandparents in wheelchairs. I want to yell, *Go away! Leave us alone! Why won't all these bad things just leave us alone?* like Buelo is yelling to the air.

Daniella is so still that I would think she was sleeping, if her lips weren't moving. I don't know what she's saying. But it looks like she's mouthing, *Why am I here?*

Buelo's room goes quiet. I stand and wait, the tray still warm in my hands. A nurse leaves the room. Mom pops her head out.

"Grab three chairs from the sitting room and come in," she says.

My heart beats fast and slow at the same time. I hold the tray in one hand and drag a chair with the other. Daniella's eyes are watery when she takes the other two chairs. She rubs her face with her shoulder, and some mascara gets on her sweater. I wish she hadn't hid the fact that she was crying. We could have stood next to each other out in the hall, instead of against two different walls.

Buelo looks sleepy when we get into his room. His eyes are half-closed. We set up the chairs in a half circle around his bed.

"We're going to have our own Family Night," Dad says. He leaves for a minute and comes back with plastic plates and utensils.

Buela opens the insulated carrier, and a strong, peppery smell fills the room. It covers up any trace of soup or sanitizing spray or sadness.

We serve ourselves big scoops of rice. Dad talks about funny customers at Holy Baloney, and Buela says the potluck would have been nothing but casseroles. I watch Daniella clear her plate and then fill it up for the second time. Her face is soft and calm now, like maybe she figured out why she's here.

Lesson Eleven of Math Olympics: You have multiple strategies in your mental toolbox. Use them.

Buelo's head bobs a little. He's smiling in his sleep. I take that as his approval for the idea I've just come up with to help Daniella.

26

Boiling Point

"Are you sure about this?" Ben asks.

I'm in my kitchen with Aaron, Jac, and Ben, along with oil, adobo, salt, and pepper.

"Daniella loves this stuff. It'll make her happy, I know it," I say. The bag of yellow rice spills out like a trail of breadcrumbs leading to the empty pot heating up on the stove.

Jac pulls on a red-checkered oven mitt and hands the matching one to Ben, even though the mitts aren't really required for making Buela's rice and peas.

"Let's do it," she says.

I stare at the rice pot and suddenly panic.

Oil + Rice + Peas = ?

Water + Adobo + Rice = ?

The order of the ingredients mixes up, like variables I never learned how to solve for. I reach for the bottle of oil and dump it into the pot. It makes a hot, splashing sound when it touches the copper.

"Have you done this before?" Aaron asks. He takes a step back from the sizzling oil.

"I've seen my Buela do it a hundred times," I answer. I try to ignore the strong smell of something burning. I add some adobo to the oil to cover up the smell.

"Well, I don't want to question your grandma, but I'm pretty sure you use water for rice," he says.

"We should've stuck to nachos," Ben sings into a wooden spoon. Jac takes a step forward and picks up the bag of rice.

"No, I think Cassi's right. Now we just add this." She tips the bag, and yellow grains go everywhere. Some make it into the lava-hot oil, but most spill underneath the burner. Black smoke floats up around the pot.

"Jac!" I shout.

"Cassi!" she shouts back.

"Aaron!" Ben joins in.

Aaron laughs too hard to say a name back, but nothing is funny. The kitchen fills with thick clouds. Some oil leaks over the edge of the pot. I turn the burner off, and a flash of heat scalds the skin on my wrist.

The smoke alarm starts wailing.

"Help me open the windows," I order. We spread out. Aaron opens the kitchen windows, and Jac sprints to open the front door. Ben waves a towel in front of the detector, moving his hips like the piercing beeping sound is a song instead of a disaster. The smoke bobs around in the air like it's dancing with him.

Daniella comes down the stairs and into the kitchen,

and takes a quick look at the damage. She rushes over to the stove and moves the pot to another burner. She strips the towel out of Ben's hands, then waves it hard until the smoke is pushed out the windows and the beeping stops.

"What are you doing?" she asks. Her voice is breathless but still sharp.

"Cooking," I answer.

Daniella's eyes fall on the line of spices and oil, the half-empty bag of rice.

"Cooking what?"

Jac waves her hand at our setup.

"It's pretty obvious, don't you think?" she says.

"Hey, Jac, can you for once, like, not?" Daniella asks. "I'm sure it was your master plan to burn the house down, anyway."

Jac's face crumples. She runs out the sliding door and slams it behind her. It's too dark outside to see where she goes from there. Ben follows her into the night. Silence falls over the kitchen. The air is thick with the smell of disappointment.

"It wasn't her idea," I say.

Daniella's eyes flicker to the sliding door and then the floor.

"Did Mom ask you to make rice, then?"

"No. I wanted to make it for you. I know it's your favorite."

Her face pinches. She studies the smoke alarm like it might go off again. Through the open windows, I can hear Jac and Ben talking outside. A cold breeze slips in with their voices.

"Well. Thanks. I guess." Her eyes shift to the window. "And tell Jac I said . . ."

Daniella's voice drifts off. She leaves the kitchen without finishing her sentence.

"This is Aaron, by the way," I call to her before she can get up the stairs. She turns around with one hand on the banister. Aaron lifts his arm like it weighs ten pounds and waves weakly.

"Hi," she says, and then she's gone.

I pour the oil from the pot into the jar mom keeps near the stove. Buela has a jar like it too. Mom says that when I have a kitchen of my own, I'll have a jar for leftover oil by the stove. But maybe I won't. I can't even make rice.

Aaron and I start to clean up the kitchen in silence, as if we're the two who yelled at one another. Maybe I should tell him a story about the Chordays and the way we used to be.

Did you see that poster of the castle on Jac's wall? I'd ask. *We used to think we could transport ourselves to the kingdom inside it. We would press our fingers into the paper, close our eyes, and wait for the wall to suck us into a place where only the four of us would live.*

Boiling Point

Aaron's face is stopped somewhere between smiling and sad. Like he'd be ready to cheer me up or cry with me, whichever I needed. I add *understands* to my set of Aaron Facts.

"So about those nachos?" he asks, going with the cheering-up approach.

I laugh a little and hand him the adobo. He puts it into the cabinet. He's tall enough to reach the top shelf. When we finish cleaning, I lead us out the sliding door. Jac and Ben sit on the steps sharing a pair of headphones. The air has an edge to it, but I guess it wouldn't be late fall in Mapleton if it didn't. I sit next to Jac, and Aaron takes the spot next to Ben. We make one line on the wide, wooden step.

"What are you listening to?" I ask.

Ben unplugs the headphones from his phone, and the song starts playing on speaker: *"I'll meet you out in Elmtown. Say you won't let me down."*

"Good choice," Aaron says.

Jac leans her weight into my side. She can act like her heart is shriveled and black all she wants. I know that it's giant, and that it cares, and that there's a little piece that's broken because of Daniella too.

The four of us sit outside for a while, under the pitch-black sky.

November 28

I get the same text message every day.

"I'm here if you need me," followed by three moon-phase emojis and a koala face.

Every day I text back, "Thanks, Jac."

I have a picture taped to my mirror of two-year-old me holding Jac for the first time. I remember thinking of her as my little doll to dress up and play house with.

Until she grew up and became the exact opposite of a little doll.

Sometimes I worry she'll end up like me, carrying something dark and forceful inside. Something that pulls other people down if they stand too close.

I don't know why she still tries, even after all the things I've said when I was too sad or tired or numb to be nice. Eventually she'll see that I'm not worth her koala emojis. And then she won't be there anymore.

27

Tourist

Dad takes Jac and me to the Mapleton Mall. The stores have giant holiday sale signs in their windows. 50% OFF (SELECT STYLES). BUY ONE GET ONE HALF OFF (EXCLUSIONS APPLY). I try not to think about the missing halves.

"I have a few things to grab." Dad reaches into his pocket. He pulls out a list and two twenty-dollar bills. "If you find these for your mom, go ahead and buy them."

"Or what about this, Uncle Paul?" Jac says. "We steal the gifts and get chased by the mall cop on his Segway."

"You could. But let's try not to."

Dad loves the holidays. He goes out before the sun comes up on Black Friday and makes Daniella and me close our eyes when he comes home with shopping bags. He takes us to see the house by Buela's condo that sets their lights to music at least twice. We celebrate Three Kings' Day in January too, because Mom says it keeps us connected to our Puerto Rican heritage. I like putting grass in front of my bedroom door for the kings' camels that are supposed to stop by.

The Last Tree Town

On Three Kings' Day two years ago, Daniella and I were in the space between our rooms. She stood with her arms crossed, studying the blue plates of tangled-up grass.

"There's not enough," she said.

"How hungry do you think these camels are going to be?" I asked, laughing. But Daniella's face stayed creased with seriousness.

"They have a long journey, Cassi. And it's our job to fuel them. We need more." She disappeared into her room and came back with two big sweatshirts and some scarves. "Put this on."

I pulled Daniella's gray Eliza T. Dakota sweatshirt over my head. She wrapped a scarf around my neck until I was bundled like a mummy.

"Follow me," she said. As if I wouldn't follow her anywhere.

We trampled down the stairs. Mom and Dad were on the couch watching Jeopardy! The living room smelled like hot chocolate.

"What are you doing?" Mom asked while we put our boots on at the front door.

"Our duty," Daniella said. She took my hand and pulled me into the yard. The night was bitter cold, and the sky was swarmed with stars. I breathed it all in—the wintery air, the pine tree strung with lights near our front door, the feeling of being on a mission with my sister.

"*Now what?*" *I asked.*

Daniella squatted down and tugged handfuls of grass out of the ground, then stuck them into the pocket of her hoodie.

"*You take some too, Cass,*" *she said. I bent down next to her and gathered my own bundles of camel food. The grass was cold but somehow still soft.*

Daniella decided our pockets were stuffed enough, so we went back inside and up the stairs. We added the new grass to the piles in front of our doors. Now the plates were so full that some of the grass spilled onto the carpet.

When we walked downstairs again, Mom had our hot chocolate ready. The four of us sat in the living room with our fingers wrapped around steaming mugs and tried to answer Jeopardy! *questions before the contestants.*

I doubt Daniella will care about the camels' well-being this year. When I woke up on Black Friday, Dad's car was still in the driveway. The house by Buela's condo hasn't put up their lights yet.

I read the list Dad gave me.

Sudoku puzzle books.

That new biography—see if Cassi knows what it's called.

Dark-roast coffee.

Things Mom needs for long days at Kindly Vines. I stuff the list into my pocket.

"I'll meet you in the food court in an hour. Call if you need anything." Dad leaves us and goes into the shoe store. If it were last year, he would have made sure I wasn't looking.

Jac and I start walking in the other direction. Tinsel snakes around the pillars, and Santa's workshop is set up on the lower level. "All I Want for Christmas Is You" plays from the speakers.

"Ben would be belting this if he were here," Jac says. She pulls off her knit hat. The static makes her hair stick straight up. Blond is starting to show through the blue, like faded denim jeans. I've been tracking the color since that day we went sledding, and so far she hasn't dyed it again.

I laugh. "He totally would."

At least some things don't change. My holiday spirit lifts. Even if we don't drink hot chocolate on the couch or rip grass from the ground under a star-studded sky, even if Buela's neighbor never puts up their musical lights, we'll still set plates for the camels outside our doors. Three feet apart.

We walk into the calendar and game store, the one that only gets set up during the holidays. It's big inside, for a store that only sells two things.

"We're looking for sudoku," I tell Jac.

"Cat calendar. Got it." She disappears into the calendar section. I roll my eyes and start searching for the activity books. They're in the back corner. A whole shelf is dedicated to sudoku. I picture Mom at the kitchen table doing a puzzle and sipping the dark-roast coffee I'll buy her. Whenever I see her like that, I'm reminded of where I get my love of numbers.

I bring two advanced-level books to the register. The cashier's name tag says BRIANA. She looks a little older than Daniella and wears a bracelet with dangly charms. I see a *B* and a flower and the Puerto Rican flag. A stand in San Juan sold ones just like it. The charms crash into each other when she reaches for my money.

"Have you ever been to El Morro?" I ask her.

"In San Juan?" Briana opens the change drawer.

"Yes. The citadel."

"No, my family's from Bayamón. San Juan is full of tourists." She holds my bag out. "Have a good one."

She's already looking at the customer behind me. I snatch the bag of sudoku books.

Jac is rearranging price stickers in the calendar section. I pull her out of the store. A little orange tab with *$9.99* sticks to her finger.

"What is wrong with you?" She presses the price sticker into my forehead.

"Nothing."

Except that when I felt most at home in Puerto Rico, I guess I was also being a *tourist*. I wish that I'd bought one of those charm bracelets with the flag, so that Briana would've known I was Puerto Rican too. So that everybody would.

I peel the sticker off my face and throw it into the garbage.

"Let's go to the coffee shop," I say.

I wait for Jac to make a comment, but she doesn't. The speakers play a holiday song with no words. We take the escalator, and I watch the first floor come into view inch by inch as we make our way down. We're wedged between a man holding a big box with the image of a blender on each side, and a couple with a small girl wearing a velvet dress. A mall in December is a good reminder of how many people there are in the world. Jac jumps off when we get to the bottom, even though it clearly says to watch your step.

"Is that Aaron?" Jac asks. We get closer to the couches arranged near the escalator. "Of course it is. He's a skyscraper."

I follow her. Aaron stands by a gray couch with a plastic Old Navy bag in each hand. He's looking toward the giant tree set up near Santa's workshop. Jac calls out his name so loud, he jumps.

"Quiet down or you'll scare the reindeer," he says.

"Don't worry. I already set them free," Jac replies.

It seems like the kind of thing that would make Aaron laugh. Instead he's quiet and looks over his shoulder. A man with a bushy brown beard sits on the couch behind him, writing urgently in a notebook.

"Dad?" Aaron says. His dad keeps writing. "Dad." He

says it more harshly than before. Mr. Kale looks up.

"Oh. Wow. Sorry. I sunk into it for a minute." He blinks a bunch of times.

"These are my friends Cassi and Jac." Aaron points to each of us.

"We aren't really friends," Jac says. I elbow her.

"Honesty is good." Mr. Kale closes the notebook in his lap. It's one of those basic red spiral-bounds that stores sell for ninety-nine cents before school starts. "Memoir Ideas" is written on the cover. It reminds me of Daniella's *Thoughts* diary.

"That's what I've been saying!" Jac smiles. The girl in the velvet dress starts crying at Santa's workshop.

"I apologize for being a bit distracted. Had to see where this burst of inspiration took me."

"The Mapleton Mall inspired you?" I ask. There are a ton more inspiring things about Mapleton than this mall. I think of the Founders' Day fireworks in June. When they shoot off the weeping-willow-looking ones, I imagine the sparks falling around me like glittering rain.

Is that inspiring? Is that something to put in a memoir? I wonder if *The Chemical Property of Life* could explain the science behind weeping willow fireworks.

"Too many people around for there to be nothing to uncover." Mr. Kale sticks his pen into the notebook's spiral binding. "Good thing. I was about ready to give up on Mapleton."

Aaron's eyes look like they could burn holes in his Old Navy bags. His hands are tight around the plastic.

"There are a lot of good things here," I say. Mr. Kale holds up the *Memoir Ideas* notebook.

"And we intend to find her." He pulls Aaron into the crook of his elbow even though Aaron is a few inches taller.

Her? He must have meant "them" or "it" or "stories."

"See you at school," Aaron mumbles as they walk away.

"See you," I say to his back.

Jac clicks her tongue. "And you say I'm bizarre." She walks toward the gourmet coffee shop. The sweet smells of caramel and vanilla slip out of its golden doors.

Mr. Kale's words repeat in my head. *Ready to give up on Mapleton.* I guess I've been too mesmerized by Aaron's stories to realize how they all end.

He leaves.

Maybe I'm not the only one who has felt like a tourist.

Winter

28

Ugly Sweaters

On the Saturday before Christmas, I sit on my bed under a blanket that has princesses and jeweled magic mirrors on it. The fleece is so worn that the princesses don't have faces anymore. Last winter on this same weekend, Daniella and I helped Buela make cookies for the soup kitchen at Saint Anthony's. The counters at the condo were covered in trays of mantecaditos, butter-colored cookies with sprinkles or guava paste on top. Daniella and I kept sneaking some when Buela's back was turned, and then rearranging them to cover up what we'd done. Buelo was watching us from his recliner the whole time. When we noticed him, he put one finger over his mouth—*Shh*. We knew he wouldn't tell.

Buela isn't making cookies this year. She's spending her Saturday at a church service in Kindly Vines's small chapel, a room with two pews and a cross on the wall. Daniella is going to a high school party.

Someone knocks on my door.

"Who is it?"

The door eases open before anyone answers. It's

Daniella. She wears a zebra print bathrobe and a towel on her head.

"Hey," she says.

"Hey." My heart thumps with surprise.

I think back to the last time she was in my room, sitting on my bed.

Head bent over my hands while she painted my nails + a waft of coconut-mint body spray + curls like a curtain falling forward = The Daniella I still try to hold on to.

"Are you busy?" she asks.

I glance at the Math Olympics workbook on my lap. It's open to a half-finished problem. *If one bird sings every twenty seconds, a second every thirty, and a third every ten, how many times will they sing together in three minutes?*

"Not really."

"Mom said to invite you to this party. You don't have to come."

I would go anywhere she invited me, even if it was Mom's idea.

"I'll come."

"'Kay. Wear an ugly holiday sweater."

She leaves before I can ask what that means. I squeeze myself into a ball so that my happiness stays in, feeling like a fourth bird in that math problem. One that sings until its lungs collapse.

—

The party is at Jenna's house, on the street next to ours, so we walk. I count the words we say back and forth. We almost reach a hundred.

"Everyone is going to wear an ugly sweater?" I ask. I picked out a red-and-white-striped sweatshirt, because it looked like a candy cane.

"Yup, that's the whole point." Daniella's sweater says "*Feliz Navidad.*"

"I'm happy to be going with you," I blurt. The words make me feel like a little kid wishing on snowflakes.

"Me too, Cass."

I imagine the wall in Daniella's chest piecing itself back together. Maybe this is what things will be like now. Instead of baking cookies we'll walk together to high school parties with themes. I guess I can get used to the fluttery feeling in my stomach.

We make it to Jenna's house. The windows look like the carved face of a jack-o'-lantern, bright but eerie. Daniella walks in without knocking. Jenna is in the front hall wearing a sweater with a stocking sewn on. Her smile fades a little when she sees me.

"Oh, hey, Cassi. Wasn't expecting you." She adjusts her short black skirt. Her tights have diamond patterns.

"Mom made me bring her. But she'll be cool." Daniella stares me down. "Won't you?"

I nod, but how can I be cool in an ugly sweater?

I bounce around with Daniella for a while, standing

quietly while she goes from conversation to conversation. At some point she leaves for the drink table and I lose her. Jenna has a cookie bar set up in her kitchen. I wander over and fill a napkin with tree-shaped sugar cookies. I try not to think about hot trays of mantecaditos on Buela's counter, Buelo watching us, Daniella and me with guava paste on our hands.

I find a spot on the couch downstairs and eat the cookies one after another. Hopefully this is what Daniella meant by being cool. The basement smells musty, and the couch cushions are covered in white cat hair.

A blond boy in a Rudolph the Red-Nosed Reindeer sweater sits next to me. Rudolph's nose is a small round bulb that flashes.

"Haven't seen you around before," he says.

"I'm Daniella's sister," I say.

He inspects my face and every stripe on my candy cane sweater. I feel trapped under a magnifying glass in the sun.

"Really? You don't look alike."

I stuff a sugar cookie into my mouth and chew until he goes away.

It tastes like cardboard.

"Let's play Spin the Bottle," Jenna announces, walking down the stairs with a soda bottle raised over her head like a trophy. She sits down near my feet, and a group forms around her. My spot on the couch makes me part of the circle. Daniella finally shows up again and sits next to me.

"I don't want to play," I whisper.

"You'll be fine," she says. "Don't you want to fit in?"

Her words stun me like a paper cut. Quick and painful. Daniella knows how much I want to fit in. She's the person who used to make me feel like I could, even if I was a bad dancer, even if my hair was frizzy. But not anymore.

"Okay. I'll do it."

Jenna explains that you have to go into the closet with the person the bottle points to. Those are the rules.

When it's my turn, I lean down from the couch and spin the soda bottle. I get dizzier the longer it twirls. It stops on the boy with the Rudolph sweater. He stands and walks fast to the closet. I don't move.

"It's just two minutes," Daniella says into my ear. "You don't have to do anything you don't want to do."

"Promise?" I ask.

"Yes." She nudges me out of the circle. I step into the closet, and the door closes behind me. It's dark and small, like the inside of a cave. The wet smell of the basement follows me. I can't see the boy.

"Can you turn the light on?" I ask.

"Sure," he says.

I hear a click, and his sweater lights up. Rudolph's

nose blinks like a stoplight, flashing across the boy's face. I'm sure the whole party can hear my heart beating. The song "Last Christmas" slips in through the space under the door. Why did Daniella tell me to do this? Why aren't we keeping up Buela's tradition and pressing rainbow sprinkles into cookie dough?

"You can come closer," the boy says.

"No, thank you." I use the light from his sweater to look around. *Lesson Fifteen of Math Olympics: If you're stuck, look at a different part of the problem.* There's a stack of board games in the corner. I sit down on Monopoly.

"We're supposed to make out." His breath smells like corn chips. I count the seconds. *It's only one hundred and twenty seconds.*

"No, thank you." The air is so thick, I can't breathe. I don't want to be cool anymore.

Someone pounds on the door.

"Time's up."

I stumble out of the closet, and the blond boy follows. The slap of a high five echoes behind me. I don't get back in the circle. I walk across the damp basement, up the stairs, and out the front door.

Daniella doesn't even try to stop me.

I forget my jacket in the pile on Jenna's bed. My sweatshirt is too thin for the cold, but I don't stop. Houses glow with Christmas lights. I want to feel the way I did when Daniella and I walked side by side to the party, like things could be better even if they were different. I can't. Snow seeps into my boots like my anger, icy and irritating. So what if the wall in Daniella's chest fell? Did she have to knock everyone else down with it?

It takes three hundred and thirty-seven steps to get to my room. The Math Olympics book is still on my bed. I throw it onto the ground. The birds will never sing together. I bury myself under the blanket with the faceless princesses.

The front door opens a while later. Daniella kicks the snow off her shoes before coming upstairs. She stops in the spot between my room and hers. My door cracks open.

"I shouldn't have brought you," Daniella whispers into the dark. I hear my jacket fall to the floor.

Luckily, the blanket is over my head, so she can't see that I'm awake. I'm afraid to close my eyes. I'm afraid of the nightmares. Of whispers and corn chips and dark closets. Of red lights that blink and then burst.

29

The Reflection

I stand at the kitchen sink, soaking my oatmeal bowl and staring out the window. Mom must have cleaned it with Windex recently. It's clear enough for me to see my reflection.

My hair is longer than it was when Daniella and I looked in the mirror at Kindly Vines. It grows as fast as weeds. The curves in my hips and chest have filled out a little more, like Mom said they might. I stand and stare at the reflection until I don't recognize who looks back.

The Reflection's eyes swim with tears. Her hair is too frizzy. Her freckles stay sprinkled across her cheeks. If someone asked her to dance like no one was watching, she couldn't. A sob gets stuck in her throat, something deep and desperate that she doesn't want her family to hear. She swallows it down.

The hot water in the sink creates steam, thick and swirling like a ghost.

Fantasma.

"Stop it," the Reflection whispers. The sound of her own voice scares her. She looks away from the window, from herself. The kitchen table is covered in birds that can't fly. It's where she eats silent breakfasts with her sister, where she filled out an application that told her who she could be. The Reflection's heart knots up.

She imagines a new kind of application. It asks: *Do you want things to be the way they were?*

She checks "Yes."

30

Five, Four, Three, Two . . .

For as long as I can remember, everyone comes to our house on New Year's Eve. Jac and Uncle Eric, Ben and his parents, and Buela and Buelo. It's tradition. But things are different this year. Buelo isn't here. Leslie is. And Daniella doesn't want to be. She sits in a chair by the tree, running her finger over a silver bell ornament, ignoring everyone.

"Try not to be miserable," Mom says. She sits on the love seat with Buela.

Daniella tilts her head and widens her mouth into a fake smile.

"Excellent." Mom blinks hard. Buela puts a hand on her leg. I swear she whispers, *"Todo estara bien,"* like Mom does to Daniella and me.

I sit on the carpet near the TV with Jac and Ben. We're watching people freeze in Times Square. It's sort of a reunion, since Ben spent the holiday two states away with his grandparents, and Jac was at her mom's. We don't have to say "missed you" to know it's true. We just sit closer together.

"Why is she acting especially angsty tonight?" Jac asks.

It's been like this since Jenna's party, I should say. But then I'll have to think about the tasteless cookies and musty basement and Daniella insisting that I'd *be cool.* I don't want to think about those things, even if it means keeping a secret from my best friends.

"I can hear you, you know," Daniella says.

Jac looks over her shoulder.

"Yeah, I know." She smiles, but it looks sad instead of scary.

"Very mature, Jac." Daniella grips the edge of her chair.

"Can everyone just take it *easy?*" Dad snaps from his recliner.

Dad never talks like that. It's always Mom who does the disciplining. But nothing is the same anymore. I try to focus on the TV instead of the tension in the room. The camera cuts to a group in matching hats that say *We traveled three thousand miles for this.*

Uncle Eric clears his throat. "Next year we go to the city with a big sign, HOLY BALONEY, HOME OF THE SRIRACHA GRILLED CHEESE," he says. He sits in the other recliner next to Dad's.

"You go right ahead. I'll be here," Dad says, his voice slipping back to normal.

"I prefer the Kim-Chay," Leslie says, and smiles

at the Chays from her spot on Uncle Eric's recliner's armrest.

"Well, nothing beats that," Mr. Chay says. His hand is linked with Mrs. Chay's.

A country singer starts to perform onstage in a puffy coat and cowboy boots. Ben stands.

"I'm going to be there one day." He starts his own choreography to the song. I realize that the song is "Elmtown."

"Yes, you sure will," Mrs. Chay says. She picks her camera up off the coffee table, one of those big, boxy ones with the giant lenses, and snaps a picture. Mr. Chay rolls his shoulders like he's trying to learn Ben's dance moves.

"First saw you when the leaves changed, sitting in that wooden chair. Lost the nerve to say that I'd go with you anywhere." Ben sings along with the performance. Mrs. Chay snaps a picture. Dad and Uncle Eric start pretending to play instruments—Dad with an imaginary guitar and Uncle Eric on an invisible keyboard. Mom and Buela sway back and forth on the love seat. Jac stands up and attempts ballet, leaping all over the living room in a flurry of faded blue hair.

Daniella even rings the silver bell ornament. I feel the tension in the living room float away.

Almost midnight + my family singing and dancing like nothing is wrong = The way things are supposed to be.

Mom hands out noisemakers and hats and plastic glasses. We all gather in front of the TV while the ball drops. It glows like a color-changing moon on its way down.

"Ten, nine, eight, seven, six . . . ," we shout together, hats on and horns ready.

I watch Daniella lean her chin into Jac's shoulder.

"Five, four, three, two . . ." she counts into her ear.

My heart swells with light like the ball's million crystals. Ben and I lock eyes and tip our pointed hats at each other. I think about the last lesson Mr. G wrote on the board before we left for winter break.

Lesson Seventeen of Math Olympics: Without numbers, there would be no New Year's.

"One."

31

Cute

There's an oddly warm day in January, the kind where fifty-five degrees feels like summer. The gym teachers bring us out to the adventure course in the woods. There's a narrow rope bridge set up in the trees, and an obstacle where you have to maneuver from one tire swing to another, and this big wooden platform where we all have to work together to make it balance evenly. It's fun in the fall when the leaves turn orange. But now the trees are bare and the ground is frozen.

Ben has the same gym period as me, but a different teacher. Our classes join together for the adventure course.

"We should get Aaron out here. He could tell us about a tree town while in an actual tree," Ben says. He points to the rope bridge. It sways a little in the wind. A pulley system hangs down from where the bridge is attached to the tree trunk higher up. The ropes get hooked to harnesses when students are up there.

"Yeah, good idea."

The truth is, I want to slow down on the tree town

stories. After that conversation with Aaron and his dad at the mall, I'm starting to realize what happens when the stories run out.

Ms. Kapinski, my gym teacher, claps a hand against her clipboard and tells us to huddle up. She wears lime-green athletic shorts. The skin on her legs is covered in goose bumps and tinted blue. I think she might have overestimated the warmth.

"We're going to do the two-person bridge walk today. One person will start on either side. You'll both walk across at the same time. Your objective is to figure out how each of you is going to get to the other side. The bridge is too narrow for both to get by at once." Ms. Kapinski speaks in hard sentences. No matter what she's saying, it always sounds like she's giving instructions. Even "Have a good day" comes out like a command.

Ben swivels his hips, bumping me. His way of saying that we're partners.

"Please don't dance up there," I warn him.

Ben's moves + rickety bridge = A fall to our deaths.

"Maybe it's the exact strategy to get across," he says.

I guess the right solution isn't always the one you think it is. Like how I thought going to that party with Daniella would bring us back together, but it didn't. Instead it's like there's a canyon between our bedrooms. The results defied all my hypotheses.

Cute

We form lines on both sides of the bridge, one partner from each set in one line and the other partner straight across. Ms. Kapinski and Ben's gym teacher clip the first pair into the harnesses, then hold the other ends of the ropes while the students start up the ladders built into the trees. The climbing is the scariest part.

Sage from Math Olympics is behind me. She taps my shoulder.

"Are you going out with Aaron?" Her voice carries. Even some of the people in the other line turn and look.

"What? No." I've never gone out with *anyone*, ever. The idea makes my skin heat up like I'm wearing a hundred sweaters on top of each other.

"You think he's cute, though, right?"

I haven't really thought about Aaron as cute or not. But I guess I wouldn't mind looking out into the woods and seeing him there. It's kind of cute when he blushes at the big parts of his stories.

"I don't know," I say.

"Good. I just wanted to make sure it was okay for me to go out with him."

My heart pauses. "He asked you?"

"No. But he will." She's still talking loud enough for the other line to hear. I can feel Ben staring at me, but I don't look over. The first pair up on the bridge is two guys from the soccer team. When they meet at the center, the shorter one squats down and lets the other climb over him. Like leapfrog without the leaping.

"Good strategy," Ms. Kapinski says. She gives the kid attached to her rope some slack so that he can climb down the tree.

I need a strategy. Not to cross the bridge with Ben, since that leapfrog approach looked effective. I need to stop Aaron from riding off into the sunset with Sage the Great.

But not because I think he's cute. I add *just my friend, just my friend, JUST MY FRIEND* to my set of Aaron Facts.

Mr. G has us silently read an article at the beginning of Math Olympics. I stare at the back of Aaron's head like it's the first time I've ever seen it. I wish this article was about how to slow my pulse down, and not the discovery of a new formula.

"Get into groups to discuss what you learned from the reading," Mr. G says. His tie has paw prints on it.

I see Sage grab on to Allie's sweater and pull her toward Aaron and me. Aaron pushes his desk next to mine, like normal. But nothing feels normal.

"Your sweatshirt is nice," I say.

Aaron looks down at his black hoodie, and then at me. "I wear this all the time."

"Yeah, I've been meaning to tell you." Heat rushes

to my cheeks and chest and everywhere else.

"Thanks." He bends the corners of the article, looking as confused as I feel. Sage and Allie stop in front of us.

"Wanna be a group?" Sage asks.

"Sure," Aaron answers.

"Great." Sage sits down, tossing her blond hair back. Her face isn't red and blotchy. Sweat stains aren't forming under her armpits. And I'm sure her head is full of better words than "Your sweatshirt is nice."

"I thought the article was fascinating," Allie says. I look at her paper. Lime-green highlighter streaks cover the whole thing. "Can you believe that math has been around for a billion years and there's still new discoveries all the time?"

Yes, this is good. We'll discuss the article, and no one will have time to ask anyone else out.

"Agreed. And I liked that the guy named the new formula after his mom, and not himself like everyone else does," I say.

"We don't have to talk about this." Sage pushes her article to the side with a purple-painted pinky. Then she leans forward onto her elbows, facing Aaron. "Are you going to the Ice Plex thing?"

Posters for the Parents and Teachers Association ice-skating fund-raiser showed up in the halls after winter break. Jac stole one to add to the poster collection in her bedroom, but she crossed out most of the words so that it just read *Parents and Teachers Are Ice.*

"I was thinking about it." Aaron turns to me. "Are you?"

I want to be as cool and calm as Sage.

"Probs," I say. I flip my hair back, but a chunk gets stuck in my ChapStick. I want to hide under my desk.

Probs? I've never used that word in my life.

"See you both there, then," Sage says, but she's not looking at me at all. I wish Daniella were here to explain why my heart feels like it's snapping in half. Last year when she and her boyfriend Mason broke up, she cried for days even though they only went out for two months. I remember thinking it was grown-up to feel that sad over a boy.

But this doesn't feel grown-up at all. It feels uncomfortable. And Aaron isn't even my boyfriend. I just don't want him to be Sage's. Then he'll start telling her his stories instead of telling me.

Allie pounds on her desk, demanding our attention. "A billion years, people! And there are still new discoveries out there!"

32

Together

Mom is at the kitchen table with Buela when I get home from school. They both have puzzles in front of them—Mom with sudoku, Buela with a word scramble. Buela's big copper rice pot is on the stove. Steam escapes from the sides of the lid.

I kiss Buela on the cheek and breathe in her powdery smell.

"Help me, *Fantasma*." She points at the word scramble. Her place mat is shaped like an owl.

"I don't want to be a ghost." The words fall like bricks.

Buela's face wrinkles. Her brown eyes darken. Mom looks up from her puzzle.

"I'm sorry. I didn't know that upset you. I will stop," Buela says.

I want to take it back. I want to take everything back. I want to rewind and stop Buelo from collecting electricity, stop the wall in Daniella's chest from falling, stop that piñata in the cafeteria from breaking into pieces. But I can't.

"It's okay, Buela," I say. I look at her word scramble. She's trying to rearrange the word "SCGHNAE." "I'll help you. But you know I'm better with numbers."

Buela wraps her arm around my waist.

"Dinner is in an hour," Mom says.

I find words inside the scramble. "Hangs." "Cane." "Sea."

"Do you want me to tell Daniella?" I ask. Mom shakes her head.

"She knows."

I watch the clouds of steam around the pot and think about my failed attempt to help Daniella. There has to be another way.

"Changes," I tell Buela, and go upstairs.

Daniella's door is still closed. I press my ear to the wood, and the seashell DANIELLA swings above my head. She's listening to a slow song about breakups that we've listened to on her pillows a hundred times. I go to my own room and keep the door wide open, remembering how Jac and Ben and Aaron and I listened to "Elmtown" outside on the deck. Even after the rice had burned.

My speaker is in the drawer of my nightstand. I wipe the dust away and sync the speaker to my phone. The breakup song is downloaded there. I press play, leaning myself against the pillows, imagining I'm sitting next to

Together

Daniella. I can still hear the song playing through her door, which means she can hear mine too. We're listening to music together again.

Even if everything else around us changes, this song won't.

33

Truth or Dare

I'm at our house with Jac and Ben, like on most Saturdays when Jac isn't at her mom's. My door is open, and every once in a while the sound of laughter slips in from downstairs, where my parents are playing cards with Uncle Eric, Leslie, and Mr. and Mrs. Chay. An apple-scented candle makes my room smell like autumn. Jac's sleepover stuff is all over my floor. Ben isn't allowed to sleep over because Mom says it's inappropriate, no matter how good a friend he is. I wonder what she'd say if she knew about the closet and the boy in the Rudolph sweater.

"What's Aaron doing tonight?" Ben asks. His script for *Bye Bye Birdie*, the spring musical, is in front of him. He found out last week that he was cast as the lead, Conrad Birdie.

"How would I know? I don't, like, keep track of him." My voice is high and nervous.

Jac puts down the video game in her hands.

"Prank call him," she says. Her eyes flash like the apple-scented candle flame behind her. She picks my phone up and puts it on my lap.

I push it off. "No way."

Jac presses it into my leg again, harder this time. "I *dare* you."

Ben laughs and turns the page of his script.

"I don't even know how to prank call," I say. The phone gets sweaty in my hand.

"Improvise. All the great actors do it," Ben says.

I don't move. My mind spins with all the stupid things I could end up saying. Jac gets a hold of my index finger and uses it to open up the keyboard.

"You have to dial star-six-seven so that it goes through as an unknown caller," she says, and then she does. "What's his number?"

"I don't memorize phone numbers," I say.

"You memorize *everyone's* phone number."

Jac's set of Cassi Facts is too long. I sigh and give her the number I memorized from our Math Olympics roster, while she maneuvers my finger around. The ringing starts. Each ring sounds louder than the last. Jac makes me press the speaker button and then finally lets go.

"Hello?" Aaron answers.

I forget everything—every number I've ever memorized, why I'm doing this in the first place.

"Is this Pepper's Pizza?" I ask.

Ben laughs. Jac puts her hand over his mouth.

"What?" Aaron sounds like he might be laughing too.

I wait for my body to evaporate into a million embarrassed particles.

"Is this Pepper's Pizza?" I ask again.

Aaron is definitely laughing.

"No. Is this Cassi?"

I hang up and drop the phone. It bounces on the princess blanket. Jac and Ben lie on their backs, hysterical. The apple-scented candle on my nightstand crackles like it finds this funny too.

"I thought you dialed anonymously," I say.

"I did," Jac says between breaths. "He must've known your voice."

The thought makes my heart pound like I'm making the prank call all over again.

Daniella's door opens across the hall. She walks out in her gray Eliza T. Dakota sweatshirt, the one I wore on that Three Kings' Day when we collected grass. She holds a blue cereal bowl. Jac stops laughing and rolls onto her stomach.

"Dani, come in," she says.

I expect Daniella to pretend she doesn't hear. Instead she steps in. "What's up?" The milk crashes around the periwinkle rim.

"Truth or dare?" Jac asks.

Daniella rolls her eyes. "I don't know, Jac."

This was normal once, the four of us knee-to-knee in

a circle, telling truths. I want Daniella to climb up into the spot between Jac and me.

I have a wall in my chest and it's broken, she'd say.

"Please pick one." Jac's jaw flexes.

"Fine. Dare."

I can't fix it.

"I dare you to explain why you don't hang out with us anymore."

The room seems to take a breath and hold it.

"I'm not answering that." Daniella hardens her grip on the cereal bowl.

Help.

She turns toward the door.

"You have to. It's a *rule.*" Jac's voice sounds like something leaking.

"What you're doing right now, Jac. And your stunt in the kitchen. And your little comment on New Year's. *That* is why I don't do stuff with you anymore," she says to the pebble CASSANDRA. She slams my door behind her. It's somehow worse than when she slams hers.

The apple scent is too sweet, and autumn is long gone. I blow out the candle. Smoke curls away in a thin, wispy line like it's trying to write a message.

"I didn't want to make her mad." Jac pokes at one of the magic mirrors on my blanket.

"We know," I say.

"And we burned that rice trying to help her." She punches the mirror this time.

I grab her hand the way she did to me to make the prank call. My head feels heavy with mathematical facts—we might never be the Chordays again.

Ben draws a star next to a line in his script.

"Here, run this scene with me," he says.

Jac looks up. "Can I do voices?"

"I'd be disappointed if you didn't."

34

An Aaron Equation

*Snort-laughing at lunch when he mentioned the prank call +
spilling juice on myself while flipping my hair + wearing a
shirt like Sage's and looking like a potato sack + a stress zit in
the middle of my forehead + more snort-laughing + writing
him a note and getting a paper cut so bad that I had to go to
the nurse = All the ways I was uncool in front of Aaron this
week.*

35

Daily Double

Mom and Dad watch *Jeopardy!* after dinner, while Daniella and I take care of the dishes. I unload the dishwasher; she reloads it. That's been our arrangement forever. I hear the host list the categories for that round's questions. "Rhyme Time. You've Got Mail. Chemical Properties." My head snaps up.

"Like your textbook," I say too loudly. Daniella puts a dirty plate on the bottom rack. Mom made steak for dinner; the plate is stained with blood.

"What?" she asks. I pull out the basket of clean utensils to unload.

"Nothing. Just. 'Chemical Properties.' Thought you had a textbook about that. That's all." I separate the utensils. Forks, spoons, butter knives, sharper knives.

"Are you going through my stuff or something?"

I put the basket back into the washer for Daniella to fill, and then take out the clean bowls. How do I explain that the title stuck in my head after I saw the textbook on her floor on the first day of school? That I've seen it in a pile on her dresser when I sneak into her room to read her diary?

"No way. I just assumed you were taking Chem."

Daniella pulls a detergent pod out of the bucket under the sink.

"Good. Because that would be pretty messed up." She pops the pod in place and sets the dishwasher to auto. She leaves the kitchen. The living room stands between her and the stairs.

"Hey, Dan, what's a kind of mail from medieval times?" Dad asks.

"I don't know," Daniella says, and keeps walking, even though I'm sure she knows it's chain mail. Mom reaches out from the couch and grabs Daniella's wrist.

"You are a part of this family. Act like it," Mom snaps.

I freeze. The stack of bowls in my hands trembles. I think about the patient way Mom used to explain Daniella's growing pains. Her voice doesn't sound so calm and understanding now. But she can't give up on Daniella before I've found the right way to help her. I need more time.

Daniella pulls her arm, but Mom keeps holding on.

"I just don't feel like playing, Mom." Daniella's voice is heavy. Maybe the weight above her head is crashing down again. Maybe she'll tell my parents about it.

"I'm only asking that you try a little harder. Can you do that?" Mom lets go of Daniella's wrist.

"Yes."

Mom nods, and Daniella flies up the stairs. Dad

watches her go, squeezing the remote. I wonder if he wishes he could press the rewind button until we're back to a night when we all watched *Jeopardy!* together.

I put the bowls in the cabinet. Maybe Mom and Dad would feel better if they knew I've been trying to fix things. They could join my team; we could all work together to bring Daniella back. I step into the living room.

My parents sit close together on the couch. Mom holds her gift from last Mother's Day—a coffee mug with a printed image of our family portrait. Daniella and I wear matching dresses and our sister smiles. Mom and Dad have their hands on our shoulders. Mrs. Chay took the photo, and then we got the mug made at the mall. Our faces look all grainy, but Mom cried when she opened it anyway.

"You're blocking the questions," Mom says.

"I need to talk to you," I say.

Mom looks at Dad, and then back at me.

"What's wrong, *mi amor*?"

My heart speeds up. I can't let Daniella hear me. I can't have her think I'm more messed up than she already does.

"Daniella needs our help," I whisper.

A siren goes off on the TV behind me. The sound for the Daily Double. Dad turns the volume down.

"We've talked about this. She's going through changes."

Mom sets the mug down on the coffee table. The day we took that portrait, Daniella and I fought on the car ride to Mrs. Chay's studio. I don't remember what it was about. Maybe that part doesn't matter. I fumed in my yellow dress and our identical San Juan sandals, and had to act happy anyway.

"It seems like more than that."

The *Jeopardy!* contestant wagers all his money on the Daily Double. If he answers the question wrong, he'll lose everything.

"It's not. You'll understand when you get to be her age," Mom says.

I already understand. I read about it in her diary. I'm too afraid to say it. I'm too afraid of how mad Daniella will be, like that day of the family portrait times a thousand.

Dad grips the remote tightly again.

"I think she has a point, Flora. It's gone on for quite a while now," he says.

Mom's eyes narrow. "I know my daughter. I've talked to her. If she needs help, she knows to ask for it. And she's not asking." Mom looks at me. "You can be sad that she's not spending as much time with you. It's okay. But she's older. Your lives are different now."

Mom seems so sure, like that contestant who picked the Daily Double and bet everything.

But I don't think she has the right answer.

36

The Ice Plex

I haven't been to the Ice Plex in forever, but everything is exactly the same. The entrance leads into a big sitting area with the skate rental booth and snack bar. A clear divider separates the sitting area from the actual rink, like the glass cafeteria wall at the high school. The whole place smells like wet socks.

Eliza T. Dakota Middle School has taken over. Sixth and seventh and eighth graders are everywhere—in line for fries and out on the ice and on every single bench. I tie up my skates next to Jac and Ben, making sure to get the laces extra tight around my ankles the way I learned in skating lessons. Ben is putting on full padding. He has knee pads, wrist guards, and a helmet.

"Explain yourself," I say, and point to the chest protector on the seat next to him. I recognize it as Mr. Chay's. He's an umpire for the town softball league. I almost expect Ben to pull a face mask out of his bag too, and the little clicker Mr. Chay uses to keep track of the strikes.

"I have a performance coming up. I cannot bruise,"

he says. Jac smiles, and I swear the air in the rink gets colder. Ben presses his lips together. "I realize now that I shouldn't have mentioned that."

Jac puts a dramatic hand over her heart and bats her eyelashes. It reminds me of how Sage has been acting toward Aaron ever since the day at the adventure course. My stomach rolls. I can see her on another bench with Allie and their friends. She's wearing a gray vest and a matching knit head wrap. Her tan socks end above her boots. I saw an outfit like that in one of those catalogs that come with the Sunday paper. It looks even better on her than on the model.

I try to convince myself that she won't steal Aaron away, no matter how trendy she is. He's my friend. He sat at the hummingbird place mat and ate Buela's tostones. Those things are important.

"Let's skate," Jac says. We waddle out of the sitting room. It's hard to walk on blades. The ice is already carved up when we get out there, but it's still smooth enough for us to glide. I feel weightless and free. I stretch my arms out like wings and tilt my head back. I forget to care about who could see me and think I'm not cool.

"I didn't know you could fly." Aaron's voice brings me back down to earth. I start to sweat even though I'm in a room full of ice.

"Yes, well, learning," I spit out.

"Maybe work on the whole *speaking* thing first," Jac suggests. She hovers near Ben, who grabs the edge of the rink with both hands.

I roll my eyes and take a deep breath of cold air. *Get it together.* Before I can try to speak a full sentence, Sage skates across the rink toward us, scraping her blades on the ice so that they make a little pile of snow. She picks up a handful and tosses it at Aaron. It splatters on the sleeve of his jacket.

"Oops. Sorry."

Please don't smile at her.

Aaron grins and starts scrounging up his own stash of snow. Sage skates away. She looks pretty even when she's squealing.

None of Mr. G's lessons have taught me how to deal with Aaron chasing after a girl with a perfect outfit on. Maybe he'll keep skating all the way to another tree town.

I creep on the two of them so long that Ben and Jac leave me behind. I do the only thing I can think of, which is copy Sage, like the Fibonacci sequence in math that repeats itself. I rub the edge of my blade against the ice until there's a powdery pile at my feet.

"Hey, Aaron." I skate toward the center of the rink with my glove full of snow.

He looks up. I throw my ice ball. It flies fast and straight. Directly into Aaron's eye.

"Agghh." Aaron holds his face. There's ice in his hair, and his jaw is clenched tight. I see Jac laughing in the background, which is how I know for sure that I've done something completely *un*funny.

"I'm so sorry," I say. I move closer, but Aaron is skating toward the exit. Sage looks at me, her cheeks rosy. Her high ponytail doesn't have bumps the way mine always do. I bet she's never doubted for a second who she's supposed to be.

"Wow, Cassi. It was just for fun," she says. She slips away with Allie.

Jac and Ben join me on the big logo at center ice. Ben looks like a beach ball with all his padding. I appreciate that he let go of the wall for me.

"Why are you going up against Sage the Great all of a sudden?" Jac asks. Hair falls out from her beanie.

"I wasn't. I was joking around."

Ben's mouth forms an *O*. It makes him look even rounder.

"This is because of what she said about Aaron!"

"What did she say about Aaron?" Jac points the tips of her skates together into the shape of a pizza slice. We learned how to do this in our skating lessons. The instructor said it was how you stop.

"That she was going to get him to ask her out," Ben explains.

Jac's mouth drops open. I wonder if the pizza-slice

method can be used to stop this conversation.

"You. Like. Aaron." I can see the jokes forming behind her eyes. How many times will I hear her sing "Cassi and Aaron sitting in a tree"? And it's not even *true*.

Is it?

"Go to him. Shakespeare once said 'love is blind.'" Ben points his elbow-padded arm at the sitting area. "And you have literally blinded him."

Aaron is alone on one of the benches, with a paper towel held to his eye.

"What if he's mad?" I ask.

Jac and Ben each take one of my shoulders and shove. I slide toward the entrance, feeling numbed by nerves and cold air, and then step off the ice. My blades dig into the rubber mat that's all over the floor. I wobble, but keep my eyes on Aaron. *Five more steps. Three more steps.*

"Hi," I say.

Aaron glances up. His face is half-covered with a paper towel.

"Hey." He looks back down at his skates.

"Can I sit?"

Please say yes.

"Are you going to attack me again?"

I hold up my hands to show I have no weapons. Aaron nods, and I sink down next to him.

"I'm so sorry, Aaron."

He pulls the paper towel away. His eye is squinted and red. It fills me with slimy regret. I add *hates me* to my set of Aaron Facts.

"You've been acting strange lately." His voice is heavy with anger, like the boy in the Rudolph sweater getting mad that I wouldn't kiss him.

My brain is a calculator with crossed wires. Is that what Aaron wants too? We're sitting close enough on the bench that I could lean in and give him the quickest kiss—my first kiss. Would that make this better? What if I'm not ready for that? I wish I could be someone who boys ask to dance, someone who's good at playing Spin the Bottle. But I'm not. I'm the one viewing from the corner. I'm the one on the couch with a napkin full of sugar cookies.

"I'll make you a deal," I blurt.

"Huh?"

"Forgive me, and I'll tell you a story."

Aaron looks at me. I want him to laugh or smile, but he doesn't.

"Okay," he says.

My face flames like I'm under a heat lamp. I take a breath.

"One afternoon, when I was ten years old, I fell off my bike. I was on Smith Street, by my grandparents' condo. I cut myself from my palms to my wrists, and my sister helped me up. She cleaned my cuts and covered them with Band-Aids that had Snoopy on them. I can still remember the way she said 'This is going to hurt' before she used the rubbing alcohol. It made me feel like I could get through anything as long as Daniella was there with a Band-Aid."

I show him the crescent-shaped scar that the fall left behind on my wrist. He doesn't say anything.

"I know I'm not as good at telling stories as you," I mumble.

"No, it's a good one," Aaron says.

He smiles. I start to erase *hates me*, but only halfway.

"I really am sorry about your eye."

"Why *did* you do that?" he asks.

My eyes drop to the rubber floor, my cheeks still burning at a thousand degrees.

"I guess I thought you might disappear unless I acted more like Sage."

Aaron taps his skate against mine. "I'd rather you were just Cassi. It seems less dangerous that way."

I laugh, and it mixes in with the screaming sound of static from the rink's loudspeaker. I replace *hates* with *forgives*. In small, secret letters, I add *cute*.

"Time for the friendship skate," a voice announces through the speaker. A song starts playing, another one I've listened to while propped up on Daniella's pillows.

"Do you want to skate?" Aaron asks. His cheeks turn the color of his injured eye.

February 14

Jenna said I should go on a double date with her
for Valentine's Day. I have no space in my brain
for heart-shaped chocolates. But I told her she
could come over before her date and I'd help her
get ready. Even though having other people in
my space feels more overwhelming every day.

She rifled through my closet and pulled out a
red shirt with a lace V-neck. She pressed it to her
body and spun around.

"What do you think? Patrick says red makes
me look like a rose," she said.

I couldn't focus on whether the shirt made her
look like a flower. A button dangled from the
sleeve by a piece of red thread.

"It's torn," I said, and pointed to the sleeve.

Jenna looked.

"Oh. I guess it is." She dropped the shirt onto
the floor and returned to the closet. She left
wearing a white sweater and lip gloss all over her
mouth.

"If you insist," I answer.

We take twelve awkward skate-steps to the rink, and then we're on the ice. Jac and Ben skate around together. Ben does disco dance moves, and Jac pretends she's going to push him over.

The song keeps playing while we skate around the rink. On our second lap, Aaron holds my hand, the laced-fingers way.

"Is that okay?" he asks.

"Uh-huh," I say, nodding. I feel the warmth from his palm even through both of our gloves.

"OH. MY. GOSH!" Jac shouts from across the rink. Her voice fills the entire Ice Plex.

I don't care about the way Sage is staring at me or if Jac makes jokes for the next fifty years, because it feels so *nice*.

Right now, I don't wish to be anyone else but me.

I picked up the red shirt and studied the broken button. Buela taught me how to hand sew and got me a kit for my eleventh birthday. I took it from its place on the dresser. I prepared the needle with red thread that almost matched the fabric. I watched it weave in and out.

But the button was tiny and I was out of practice. It hung sideways, so choked up with thread that it didn't even look like a button anymore. And that is when I stopped trying.

Jenna texted me a picture of the Dove chocolate truffles and stuffed kitten that Patrick gave her.

I thought about asking for help.

Instead I texted back, "Precious."

37

Gifts

The day after Valentine's, I'm in Ben's living room with Jac, Aaron, and Ben. His town house is the same as Jac's except opposite, like a reflection in a mirror. The coffee table is painted bright blue. Some of Mrs. Chay's photos hang on the walls, and some are clipped to clothespins on a string across the doorway to the kitchen. My favorite is in a frame next to the TV. It's of all of us at one of our summer barbecues, the Chords and the Chays, waving from a long picnic table. Mrs. Chay had set her camera up on a tall tripod. I can see Mrs. Chay in the kitchen now, cutting into pieces of pink paper with scissors.

"I brought gifts," Jac says, and tips over her backpack. Wrapped chocolates fall onto the crocheted carpet. A shiny gold bag follows behind. Aaron and Ben lunge for the stash. I stare at the trail of buttons on Jac's flannel shirt and think about the entry in Daniella's diary. Maybe there isn't room in my brain for heart-shaped candy either. It's too stuffed with worry. I pick up the gift bag and twirl the thin handle around my finger tight, my thoughts knotted up in red sewing thread.

"Where'd you get this?" Ben asks.

"I have many secret admirers, Ben," Jac says.

Ben narrows his eyes suspiciously and then starts to juggle three pieces of chocolate. I tug on the gift bag again. The little tag slides down the handle.

To Leslie. So glad I met you.

"Jac! You stole this from your Dad." I toss the gift bag at her. She smiles. The bag falls off her lap like it might scurry under the blue coffee table.

"So that's why it tastes like guilt," Aaron says. He swallows.

I laugh, and he looks at me. We're sitting next to each other on the carpet, only inches away from holding hands again. Maybe there is a little room left in my head to think about that. And to hope that my French braid isn't frizzing. I started over three times to get it perfect.

"It's not like it mattered anyway. Dad just went out and bought her a *bigger* bag of chocolates," Jac says. Ben stops juggling and puts one of the chocolates on Jac's knee.

Mrs. Chay walks in from the kitchen with a stack of pink and red paper and a box of candy hearts.

"Your dad is very happy, Jac," she says. "You should be happy for him too." I'm used to her being an extra participant in our conversations, like Buela, but I don't mind because Mrs. Chay gives good advice and Buela makes tostones. They're both honorary Chordays.

Jac unwraps the chocolate from Ben and sticks it into her mouth. "I know."

"Happy Valentine's Day, all," she says. She hands Jac, Ben, and me one of the papers from her stack. I study mine. A picture from New Year's is glued to the pink sheet—Ben and Jac and me standing in front of the TV, the streamers on our noisemakers blown straight out, Daniella standing behind us with a smile on her face and a pointed hat on. My throat constricts, tight with tears. I don't know if they're happy or sad.

Ben holds his picture up to Aaron. He's in the middle of a dance move.

"I was singing 'Elmtown,'" he explains.

"I can tell," Aaron says. He has no picture in his hands.

"You'll have to start coming around more, Aaron. Be a part of the photo shoots." Mrs. Chay hands him the box of candy hearts.

"That's not going to work, Mrs. Chay. See, Aaron is a vampire. And vampires don't show up in pictures," Jac says.

"False." Ben shakes his head. "So false."

Aaron smiles and tears open the cardboard box. Mrs. Chay laughs. Her laugh is like a camera going off. A fast, bright flash. She has one valentine left in her hands.

"This is for Daniella," she says. She gives me the red piece of paper. The same picture as mine is stuck on.

"Thanks," I say softly. I stare at it for a second, allow my eyes to trace over the words Mrs. Chay wrote underneath the picture. *We love you.* I set the paper down next to mine.

"I hope she likes it." Mrs. Chay turns to walk out of the living room. She picks her camera up off the table and heads out the door to the backyard.

I'm quiet while Jac reaches for the remote to turn on another episode of the ghost documentary. We only have three episodes left. I read the title of the one Jac just turned on—"What's Done Is Done, Or Is It?" Ben and Jac debate which episode has been the best, while the intro music starts. Jac thinks it was the one with the apple orchard. Ben says it was the one with the haunted movie theater.

I really hope this series doesn't get renewed for another season.

Aaron nudges me lightly with his shoulder.

"Here." He shakes his cardboard box.

I hold out my hands and let him pour candy hearts into my palms.

I knock on Daniella's door. There's no music inside tonight. She cracks the door open slowly.

"What's up?" she asks. Only the bedside lamp is on in

her room, and the hall light is off, so I can barely see her.

"I have something for you from Mrs. Chay." I hold up the red piece of paper with the picture. She opens the door wider. I hand it to her.

"It's from New Year's," I say.

Her eyes scan the photo. For a second, I'm scared. What if the red paper reminds her of the rose-colored shirt with the torn button?

"That's sweet." She keeps looking at the picture and not at me.

I wait. I want to see if she'll put it on the mirror with her other pictures. I want her to read the words and realize that we all still love her.

She looks up.

"Your hair looks good," she says.

I took out the French braid before bringing Daniella the valentine. It's a big, bumpy mess now, but I didn't try to fix it. It's like a lion's mane.

"Thank you," I say.

I want to tell her about Aaron and the Ice Plex and the candy hearts. But her door closes before I can, the seashell DANIELLA swinging side to side, the real Daniella out of sight.

38

Bingo

We're at Kindly Vines on a Dad-Visit Thursday, playing bingo in the recreation room. The windows look
onto the patio like a cruel reminder that it's too cold to
be outside.

"B-seven," the caller says. The room fills with the
shuffling sounds of people marking their cards with
stampers. I like bingo, because of the numbers. But I
don't have B7 on my card.

"Look, *tu tienes*," Buela says, and points to Buelo's
card. She sits on one side of his wheelchair, and I'm on
the other. He has a green stamper in his hand.

"I know." He presses his stamper into the card and
leaves a round, inky spot. Before I can stop myself I'm
thinking about my classroom nightmare. The poster
with the colored circles and the teacher telling me I
wasn't Cassi. I squeeze my stamper. I don't want to
think about the nightmare teacher while I play bingo
with my family.

"G-fifty-six."

I mark the number on my card. Buelo has it on his

card too, but Buela has to remind him again to stamp it. Mom and Dad are sharing a card. Their stamps make an *X* in the middle. Daniella puts a mark on G56. She doesn't press hard enough, so her circle is incomplete. I look away.

"You almost have bingo," I tell Buelo. He looks at me and smiles slowly.

"If I win, we split the prize?" he suggests.

"*Sí, un equipo,*" I say. A team.

One of the nurses stops in front of us then with a tray of plastic cups full of popcorn. She wears scrubs the color of pink cotton candy.

"That's very impressive that you know Spanish," she says.

My skin gets hot. "Why shouldn't I know Spanish?" I ask. "This is my grandpa."

"Cassi," Mom says in a low voice.

"Is it surprising that I could actually be Spanish and speak Spanish?" I'm causing a scene. My family is staring at me. The bingo caller up front pauses, the ball for the next number in his hand. He clears his throat.

"I-twenty-one, everybody. I-twenty-one."

The nurse puts an extra popcorn cup in front of me.

"I'm sorry, sweetie." She takes her tray to the next table.

I stamp I21 on my card. The ink smell makes my head hurt, or maybe it's the anger trapped inside, or maybe it's because things don't add up the right way anymore.

"What was that about?" Mom asks.

"Nothing," I say. The waves in my hair from the other night have gone limp. I was wrong to think that I could be a lion.

"She didn't mean anything by it, Cass," Dad says around Mom's shoulder. Daniella is looking at me too, her eyebrows pulled together.

Lesson Twenty-One of Math Olympics: Functions take something in (the input), and then give something out (the output). They're cool that way.

Maybe the nurse didn't mean anything. Maybe Daniella didn't either. Or Briana from the mall. Or Aaron when he first met me. But I'm sick of taking all these things in. I don't have anything left to fight back with.

"B-twelve," the caller says.

None of us have the number. Buelo leans in close to my ear.

"Take me home," he whispers.

I wish I could.

39

Factorials

Mr. G has us act like we've already qualified for Regionals, even though we won't find out for a few more weeks.

"I think you have a good shot," he says. He pretends to shoot a basketball into the digits of pi. His tie says GO 4 1+. "Regionals requires us to have a specialist in the speed round. The specialist is the only one who will compete in that round. Today, we'll figure out who our specialist will be."

Mr. G pulls a stopwatch out of his desk. I think about the fast math I've been doing in my head lately—the equations to help Daniella, the number of times I've wondered if Aaron would hold my hand again. The number of good moments with Buelo that cancel out the bad ones at Kindly Vines. It's all been practice for this.

"We'll pick a specialist and an alternate. Keep in mind that you're not competing against each other. You're still a team. Everyone has their own strengths, and you'll all have your chances to shine even if you're not the speed specialist."

Factorials

Markus walks to the front of the room to go first. Mr. G sets the stopwatch.

"Two hundred ninety-one plus eight hundred seventy-three," Mr. G says.

Markus hesitates, but only for a second. "Eleven hundred sixty-four."

"Correct. Twenty-two times five."

After Markus has answered five questions, Mr. G checks the stopwatch.

"One minute and fifteen seconds is the time to beat," he says. We all clap for Markus, because that's what teammates do.

Aaron leans in closer to me.

"Did I ever tell you about how I became speed specialist?" he asks.

I smile at my desk. My heart is still sore from what happened during bingo at Kindly Vines, but Aaron helps. Like the Snoopy Band-Aid that Daniella put on my cuts.

"I thought you only told true stories," I say.

Sage heads for the front of the class. She turns around in time to see Aaron with his face close to mine. Her hands fold into fists.

"What is six to the power of three?" Mr. G asks.

"Two hundred sixteen." Sage answers the next four questions in one minute flat. Her eyes stay fixed on me the whole time.

Aaron answers his questions in one minute and five seconds. Allie gets stuck on a hard question with fractions and takes almost two minutes. I clap a little extra. Emilio finishes in one minute and two seconds, just barely losing to Sage.

I'm the last one up. I take the spot at the front of the classroom. Mr. G raises his stopwatch and presses go.

"Five as a factorial," he says.

I remember *Lesson Eighteen of Math Olympics.*

Factorials multiply every positive number that comes before the integer. P.S. Don't forget to shout about it with a !

So 5! would equal five times four times three times two times one.

"One hundred twenty," I say.

Mr. G fires question after question, and I answer them faster than I knew I could. I feel made of math. He presses the button on the stopwatch.

"Fifty-six seconds. We have our speed round specialist." Mr. G hands me the stopwatch like it's a blue ribbon. Everyone claps except Sage, our alternate.

I walk back to my desk thinking maybe I'm a factorial. All the things that have happened to me before get multiplied inside my heart, and make up who I am.

40

Writing on the Wall

I sleep over at Jac's on Thursday. It's just the two of us tonight. School-night sleepovers always feel different from normal ones, maybe because it's harder to convince our parents to let us do it, or maybe because I have to pack my textbooks along with my toothbrush. The sun is staying up in the sky longer, so a hazy light filters in through Jac's living room windows.

"We need darkness for this," Jac says. She kneels on the couch and closes the navy-blue curtains.

"That's a myth," I say. "It's scary whether it's dark or not."

Jac pulls up another episode of the documentary series. I read the title. "A Family Portrait." Nerves poke at my stomach.

"Can't take any chances," she says.

"Won't Ben be mad if we watch while he's at rehearsal?"

"It's not the finale, so it's fair game."

Don't watch the finale of anything without each other + don't put guacamole on the nachos = Fundamental Chorday rules.

I'm out of escape plans. The episode starts. The narrator is an interior designer who moved into an old house to flip it. There was this wall in the house with hideous striped wallpaper that she wanted to tear off. A family portrait was hung on the wall, but the designer didn't think too much of it. She took it down and used a steaming machine to remove the wallpaper. But the portrait was back on the wall the next morning, except the grandma in the family was missing, like she'd crept out of the picture and into the house. The designer took down the picture again and threw it into the dumpster outside, but the same thing happened the next day. Only this time the sister was gone.

"I need to put sweatpants on," I say, palms slick, heartbeat out of control.

"Watch out for Luna."

The ghost-sister's name was "Luna." My skin crawls.

"You're the worst." I walk up the stairs and into Jac's room at the end of the hall. I look around, unsure of what I'm really doing in here, like the first time I snuck into Daniella's room. There aren't even sweatpants packed in my bag. I just wanted to get away from those ghosts.

I sit on Jac's camouflage comforter. Her walls are forest green, but the only place you can tell is on this one strip next to her bed. The rest is covered in posters. The poster with the castle is near the door, and the scribbled-up Ice Plex flyer is by her dresser. I climb off the bed and lie on my stomach in front of the one spot where you can see paint.

"The Chordays" is written there, in bubble letters above our names. Daniella drew a flower next to hers. There's a multiplication sign next to mine, a skull next to Jac's, and a music note next to Ben's. Doodles that show the way our minds work.

"You missed the best part."

I look over my shoulder, still stretched out on my stomach. Jac is standing at the door.

"Your dad was so mad, but he never made us paint over it," I say.

Jac pads across the carpet and sits cross-legged next to me.

"I think he knew we were just having fun," she says.

I trace the tear-drop petals on Daniella's flower.

"Do you think she'll ever be the same again?" I ask.

Lesson Twenty-Three of Math Olympics: It's okay to be scared of big numbers.

Jac tips over so her head is on my back. I think of the square, sequined throw pillow on Daniella's bed.

"I know she will."

Spring

41

Diamonds

Daniella is eating a bowl of oatmeal in the kitchen when I get home from school. A tower of textbooks sits next to her. *The Chemical Property of Life* is on top. I blink to make sure I'm not seeing things.

"There's a letter for you," she says, and points to the stack of mail on the counter.

The off-white envelope is addressed to Cassandra May Chord, which makes it seem important. In the top left corner, there's a shield with the words "Hispanic Society of Mapleton County" scripted inside.

I open it carefully and pull out the letter.

Dear Cassandra,

Felicidades! You have been selected for an academic achievement award from the Hispanic Society of Mapleton County! Each year, educators nominate distinguished Hispanic students in each of the core academic areas. You have been nominated and chosen as an honoree for mathematics.

We are proud of your accomplishments. You bring pride to the Society and the Hispanic community at large. Please join us for the award ceremony on May 1 at 5 p.m.

Sincerely,
Frank Mercado, President,
The Hispanic Society of Mapleton County

"Junk mail?" she asks.

"I won an award." I go to the table to show her. She sits at the blue jay place mat, which is usually Mom's spot. "From the Hispanic Society of Mapleton County."

Maybe this will make her see. I'm Hispanic enough for springtime ceremonies and fancy envelopes and mysterious award nominations, even if I don't look like I am.

"Cool," she says. She stirs a clump of cinnamon into her oatmeal. I wonder if she remembers asking me to be cool at the party. I wonder if she's forgiven me for not being able to.

The kitchen is quiet except for Daniella's spoon swirling around in her bowl. I sit in front of the parrot place mat. I unzip my backpack and pull out my Math Olympics workbook slowly, like any sudden movement will scare her away. My eyes are pulled to her textbooks.

"Which chapter are you on in *The Chemical Property of Life?*" I ask.

The cover is a picture of a piece of coal. Daniella puts

a hand on the book, and her fingers graze the edge of the rock.

"'Heat of Combustion,'" she says.

"What does that mean?" I ask.

"I haven't really been paying attention."

Does she think no one has been paying attention to her? Does she think I don't need her? Because if she knew, *really knew*, how sometimes I miss her so much that I can't breathe, maybe it would be enough to bring her back.

"Dani, I—"

"I'm a little tired, Cass." She puts her bowl in the sink and walks away without her textbooks. I hang my award letter on the fridge with a magnet and go back to my math problems.

The lump of coal on *The Chemical Property of Life* stares at me. When coal is put under enough pressure, it can turn into a diamond. I sit at the kitchen table while the sun sinks lower in the sky outside, and wait for Daniella to come back for her books.

I'll tell her then. I'll explain that I know about the wall in her chest, and the bad music at homecoming, and how the sensors on the school sinks don't work. I'll even tell her how I found out. She'll be so mad at me for reading her diary, so mad that the whole house might fill with pressure. But maybe that's what we need to end up bright and shiny.

I breathe deep.

"I'm going to do it," I tell the parrot place mat. "I'm brave enough to do it."

Daniella doesn't come back down for her books.

42

On Paper

Mr. G has his head down on his desk when I get to Math Olympics. Everyone who's already there looks perplexed. I take my seat next to Aaron.

"Is he sleeping?" I ask him.

"It's hard to tell," he answers. "Emilio threw a balled-up piece of paper at him, and he didn't even move."

I snap my head toward Emilio.

"You threw something at a teacher?" I ask.

"It was a desperate situation," he answers. Markus nods in agreement over Emilio's shoulder. Sage and Allie, in front, look nervous too.

Suddenly Mr. G stands. He crosses the room and slams the door shut. The digits of pi on the wall shake. I grip my pencil so hard, I'm worried it'll crack. We remain silent while Mr. G stands in front of the class, staring us down like a hawk. There's a reason why we don't have a hawk in our set of bird place mats. They're intimidating.

"I am very upset," Mr. G says. In my head, Jac's voice

says, *No duh.* "Because I cannot teach you today."

"Why not?" Allie asks, her voice wobbly.

Mr. G scoffs. He walks back behind his desk and crouches down. When he emerges, he has a box of cookies in one hand, and a bottle of lemonade in the other.

"I cannot teach you"—he slams the snacks down onto his desk—"because we have to celebrate!"

Last summer, I went to an amusement park with my family. Mom said the bumper cars gave her whiplash from colliding in so many different directions. This must be how she felt.

"We're going to Regionals!" He pumps his arm.

I shoot out of my chair with everyone else. We spin and jump and shout. Even Sage hugs me like the Ice Plex never happened. I picture big stages and bright spotlights, a silk banner that says REGIONAL CHAMPIONSHIPS.

Mr. G doesn't have us do any work for the rest of Math Olympics. Instead we polish off the cookies (somewhat smashed from Mr. G's theatrics) and lemonade and play Rummikub in teams, because even if we're taking the day off, we all still love games with numbers.

Mr. G lets us out when the late buses arrive. I pack up my backpack, but slowly. There's something I have to do. Aaron gets ready to walk out the door, but sees me hesitating.

"Aren't we going to Jac's?" he asks.

"I just have to talk to Mr. G for a second. I'll meet you on the bus."

Aaron leaves, and soon it's just me and Mr. G. He's in the middle of erasing his unused lesson from the board. *Lesson Twenty-Five of Math Olympics: Learn to simplify. Why make things harder than they need to be?*

"Mr. G?" I ask.

He turns around. His tie is covered in bananas.

"What's up, Cassi?"

"Did you nominate me for the Hispanic Society award?"

He gives me two thumbs-up. "They sent me an email to say you'd won. Congratulations."

"How did you know I was Hispanic?"

"It's public information. On your records."

I deflate, like I wasn't just part of a victory party with snickerdoodles and Rummikub.

"Oh. I thought maybe you could"—my voice catches—"tell."

Mr. G hops up to sit on his desk and moves some folders over. He taps the spot next to him. I take it. We sit with our legs dangling like we're way up high.

"You know, whatever your nationality may be, it's not about what you look like, right? Or what you are on paper. It's what's inside." He puts a hand on his chest. "I'm sure being Hispanic has impacted you in lots of ways."

On Paper

I think about the citadel, the cobblestone streets, Buela's rice. The way I'm Buelo's *corazónita*. The little figurines from Titi Celina. How warm I felt in Mayagüez. I can still feel it.

"It has," I say.

"And winning this award, it's one more way that being Hispanic changed your life." Mr. G says.

I scrunch up my forehead.

"I think I'm just getting a certificate," I say.

"Okay. Admittedly, it might not change your life, but it's still pretty awesome."

Something pounds against Mr. G's window, and we both startle. Jac's face is pushed up against the glass. Her nose is flat and her eyes are squished. She slides down the window, leaving a cloudy smudge behind.

"That cousin of yours is something else," he says.

"That's the simplified way to put it," I reply, and point to the half-erased Lesson Twenty-Five on the board. Mr. G pretends to wipe a tear away.

"My lessons are really making a difference."

43

Pudding Cup

I sit in Buelo's room with my family. Buela is in the rocking chair, Mom sits on the window ledge, and Daniella and Dad and I dragged chairs over from the sitting room. I'm working on my bio for the Hispanic Society award. It's due next week, on the day of the Math Olympics Regionals.

> *Name: Cassandra May Chord*
> *Nickname: Cassi*
> *School: Eliza T. Dakota Middle School*
> *Subject of award: Math*

"What are you working on?" Buelo asks. He takes a scoop of chocolate pudding. A new balloon hovers over the bedside table. It looks like aluminum foil and says BEST WISHES.

"It's a biography for an award I won," I say.

"My *corazónita* won an award?" His glasses lift when he grins.

"From the Hispanic Society of Mapleton County, Papi." Mom glances at me from the window ledge, looking proud.

Pudding Cup

"That's beautiful," Buela says. She has two knitting needles in her hands, winding through blue yarn. She's making a scarf for a donation drive at Saint Anthony's. Last year she made socks.

"What questions are on there?" Buelo asks.

"Normal ones. My hobbies, what school I go to, my name," I say.

He laughs. Some pudding falls off his spoon back into the plastic container.

"How would I answer that question? Pico or Eduardo?"

Buelo, lively, eating a pudding cup + the Eduardo Story = Remembering.

"What do you mean, Buelo?" I push my chair closer to the end of his bed. Daniella looks at me. Buela smiles over her knitting needles.

"Haven't I told you about the day my name was changed?" Buelo asks.

"Will you tell the story again?" I ask. Buelo puts down the pudding cup. He straightens up in his bed.

"*Sí.*"

He tells the whole thing, not skipping a single detail. How he walked to school on dirt roads with Titi Celina. How after only an hour, he had a brand-new name. How he had to learn to write "Eduardo" on lined paper.

He pauses in the same places to wait for our reactions. I look at Daniella, and she's smiling. The silver *Best Wishes* balloon sways like the kite at the citadel.

"That can't be true, Buelo," we say together.

"I mean it." Buelo nods. "I mean it, *corazónitas*."

44

Bye Bye Birdie

I sit in the dark Eliza T. Dakota auditorium between Jac and Aaron, watching Ben become a different person onstage. His character is a music sensation who gets drafted into the army. My favorite part in any of Ben's plays is when they end. Not because the shows are bad or anything. It's the moment when the curtains swing back open and Ben takes a bow. His smile is big enough for the back row to see. I think that's what it looks like when a person is doing exactly what they're meant to be doing.

When the show is over, we all file out of the auditorium. My parents were sitting in the row behind us with Uncle Eric, Leslie, and Mr. and Mrs. Chay. Yellow daylight fills the lobby, and I rush to shield my eyes. I forgot what day or time or year it was in the real world. I was still hovering somewhere in the 1950s with Ben/Conrad Birdie. The sun makes checkerboard shapes on the floor.

"Wasn't he stunning?" Mrs. Chay asks us. She has her camera strapped around her neck. I wonder if it's hard for her that flash photography is forbidden in the theater.

"He sure was," Uncle Eric says. He takes Leslie's hand.

"PDA is not allowed on school grounds," Jac says.

"Okay, Jac."

"It isn't! Consult the student handbook." She looks around the circle for support but doesn't find it. Leslie half smiles, her face full of patience. Maybe she's gotten used to Jac's commentary the way the rest of us have.

Ben comes over to our group with his face caked in stage makeup. Someone made his thick, brown eyebrows even thicker with paint, so they look like giant pine cones. Mr. and Mrs. Chay smush him into a group hug.

"My Birdie," Mrs. Chay says. When his parents release him, Ben's stage makeup is smeared on their shirts. They don't seem to mind.

"Good work, pal." Dad fist-bumps Ben.

We all take turns complimenting the star, and then the group separates in two—twelve-year-olds and adults.

"You were really good," Aaron says. His program for the play is folded into a paper plane.

"Thanks, Aaron." Ben is still smiling just as big as he did during the bows. I imagine him turning into a balloon and floating straight up to the ceiling.

"I much preferred your performance as a sheep in *Little Bo Peep*," Jac says.

"That was in first grade."

Jac shrugs, but she doesn't fool Ben or me. She has the programs from all Ben's shows taped to her wall.

"Daniella didn't come?" Ben asks. At his last show, Daniella gave Ben a big bouquet of roses. She held them in her lap the whole time. I sat next to her, breathing in the sweet scent of the flowers.

"She had to study. Sorry," I say, though all she really said was no.

"It's fine." His smile droops a little.

Over Ben's shoulder, I can see Mr. Kale walking toward us. At least I think it's Mr. Kale. His beard is gone.

"Is that your dad?" I ask.

Aaron turns.

"Yeah." He stuffs his paper plane into his pocket and waves. "He wanted to pick me up. We're going story hunting."

"What equipment is required for story hunting?" Jac asks.

"A spear."

Mr. Kale joins our circle. The red *Memoir Ideas* notebook is tucked under his arm.

"I remember you." He points at Jac. "The honest one."

Jac bows like *she* was the one who just finished a performance.

I introduce Mr. Kale to my parents and Uncle Eric,

Leslie, and the Chays, and for a second I can picture it. Aaron and his dad never leave for another tree town. We set more places at the picnic table for our summer barbecues. Aaron sits with us at the edge of the pool at Lakeside Townhouses, and we all watch the water glide over our shins. Daniella, too.

"We'll be off now," Mr. Kale says. "Stories don't write themselves."

I watch Aaron cringe and walk away with his dad. They're headed for the door when Mr. Kale suddenly veers toward a woman in a long gray sweater. He taps her on the shoulder, and then stretches out his arms as if he's going to bear hug her. The *Memoir Ideas* notebook drops to the floor.

The woman in the gray sweater backs away from him, eyes wide. Her back presses into the wall. Mr. Kale stumbles into Aaron, who pulls him out the door. Mr. Kale's mouth forms apologies as he fumbles for his notebook and they leave.

No one else seems to notice. Jac is busy rubbing her thumb across Ben's pine cone eyebrow until it looks like he has a black eye. And the adults are focused on their conversation.

I don't know who Mr. Kale imagined the woman in the gray sweater to be, but it messes with my head, because later I swear I see Daniella riding away from the lobby on a bike, curls lit up by the sun.

Bye Bye Birdie

That night when I know she's at Jenna's, I sneak into Daniella's room to read her diary. I keep the lights off. Her bed is all made up, the pillows stacked into their tower. The square sequined one sparkles on top. Daniella keeps the diary in the top drawer of her nightstand now, but something stops me before I make it there. I pick up the folded piece of paper on her bed.

Eliza T. Dakota Middle School presents Bye Bye Birdie.

She was there. She *wanted* to be there. Maybe we could be the Chordays again after all. There has to be something more I can do. To have her sit in our row of the auditorium again with roses in her lap.

I look around. My eyes find the quote calendar on her dresser. It's still stuck on the same day in July. I need to tug Daniella out of the past, out of the days when she was sad. I walk over to the calendar and rip the pages off in big clumps. Days and weeks and months tear out into my hands with sharp, slicing sounds. I try not to read the quotes. I try not to think about Daniella being angry that I snuck into her room.

She won't be angry, I tell myself. *She'll be glad that we've made it out of the bad times.*

I take the stack of calendar pages to my room and hide the days in the drawer of my nightstand, where they can't hurt anyone anymore.

45

Regionals

We take a bus to Regionals at Trinity Prep, a private school a few towns over from Mapleton. Aaron sits in the seat behind me. I look out the window. It's split into two stacked segments like they usually are on buses, but I've never noticed how the bottom panel is more zoomed in than the top one. It's the same view but different perspectives.

I feel the back of my seat move when Aaron leans over it.

"Do you ever feel like you're watching two movies at once?" he asks.

"What do you mean?" I turn all the way around in the seat. There's writing on the gray leather. A heart with two names written in it. A phone number. The words "I was here."

"Like there's two screens in front of you, and on one you're seeing what's happening now but the other screen is different. It's showing a memory or something your imagination made up." He points to the divided window like it might help prove his point.

Regionals

My heart beats faster. Had I been thinking about the window in my head, or screaming it out loud?

"All the time," I answer. "It's like I can connect everything that happens to something else."

Aaron turns away from the window and looks at me.

"Me too. It must be our keen mathematical minds."

He gets out of his seat and sits next to me. The bus runs over a branch in the road, and the bump pushes us closer together.

I wonder if *The Chemical Property of Life* explains gravitational pull.

The competition is in the auditorium. Five tables are set up on the stage, surrounding the moderator's podium. Our table is on the left side. A big index card taped to the front says ELIZA T. DAKOTA MIDDLE SCHOOL MATH OLYMPICS, and there's a name tag and program on each metal folding chair. My chair is at the end of the table, closest to the audience. I scan the program for the names of the four other schools competing. Only one of us will make it to States.

"Huddle up," Mr. G says, and we do. "You deserve to be here. Be proud of yourselves, and do only your best. That's all I could ever ask of you." There's no joke in his voice or funny look on his face. He's being serious.

Determination settles beneath my skin. I want to do well for Mr. G, who still believed in me after the first assessment catastrophe. I want to do well for my teammates. I look out into the auditorium. The lights are still on, and the red velvet seats are starting to fill. I can't find my parents or Daniella in the crowd. But I know they'll be here. I want to do well for them, too.

Mr. G leads us through some warm-up problems until the moderator taps the microphone. The sound startles everyone.

"Sorry," he mumbles. "Welcome to the Math Olympics Regionals. Let's get started."

Mr. G gives us all a thumbs-up and then goes to sit with the other coaches. The lights in the auditorium dim. I take one last look out and hope to find my family before the audience disappears, but it gets dark too fast.

"We'll start with the timed questions," the moderator says. "These questions resemble those on the assessments you've completed. My assistant is passing out the question, and on my mark, you will flip it over and work as a team to solve it. There are three minutes allotted per question, and five questions total." After each team has the question, he adds, "Good luck, and go."

Sage turns the question over.

If one cook flips a pancake every 10 seconds, a second flips every 20 seconds, and a third every 30 seconds, how many times will the cooks flip a pancake together in 5 minutes?

A light goes off in my head.

"It's the bird problem," I say.

"The what?" Allie's eyes shift toward the clock. *Two minutes and twenty-six seconds left.*

"In the workbook, there's a problem like this but with birds."

"Great. What was the answer?"

My stomach sinks. I never solved the problem. My teammates stare at me.

Aaron takes one of the allowed pieces of scratch paper and starts to draw straight lines.

"We'll make a time line," he says. He breaks the line into ten-second increments and circles the spots where each cook flips his pancake.

I think of the past few months as a time line. The night of the ugly-sweater party, the same night I saw the bird problem, would be way at the beginning. On this side of the time line, things are better. Daniella smiles, and Buelo tells stories. I can find the solution.

We count up the places where the circles line up, and bring our answer (once per minute, five times total) up to the moderator.

When the timed-questions section ends, we've gotten all of them right. The lights in the auditorium brighten, and the audience comes into view again. I scan the whole place, all the way up to the balcony, but I don't see my family anywhere. I'm not sure whether to be disappointed or worried, so I settle on both.

"There's a ten-minute break before the speed round," Mr. G says. "Go stretch your legs and hydrate. You are athletes, after all." He sounds proud. His tie has that picture of Albert Einstein with his tongue sticking out.

I walk off the stage and out of the auditorium, and grab my phone out of my backpack outside the door. We had to leave our things out on a table so that we couldn't use any devices during the competition. I look down. Messages from Jac and Ben stack up on the screen. I read the first few.

Jac: DO NOT GO ON SOCIALS.

Ben: Sorry, Cassi.

Jac: SERIOUSLY, CASSANDRA, DON'T DO IT TILL COMP IS OVER.

Ben: We can make the world's biggest plate of nachos.

Jac: PLEASE.

Jac should know better than anyone else that being told not to do something makes you want to do it more. I close out the messages and open the first app I see. My hands shake so hard, I almost drop my phone.

First I see a picture that Buela posted—three kittens in a basket. I don't think that's what Jac was warning me about. Then I see the video. The caption says *when you totally lose it*. A preview shows Daniella in the corner of a classroom. I think about the nightmare with the shell I couldn't reach and the circles of Spanish colors on the wall.

I don't even have to press play. The video starts automatically, and when it's over, it repeats.

Naranja. *Orange. The color of the desks in Daniella's American Studies classroom.*

"Daniella, I asked you a question," Ms. Murphy said. "In what year was the Declaration of Independence signed?"

Daniella stayed quiet, stared down at the desk.

"In what year was the Declaration of Independence signed?" Ms. Murphy repeated, her voice firm.

Daniella stood from her chair in the back corner and pushed the desk over. Rojo. *Red. The color of her face.*

"Stupid. Stupid. It's all stupid." Her voice was clear, even though whoever recorded the video was across the room.

Amarillo. *Yellow. The patch of sun Daniella dashed across to reach the bulletin board in the back of the class.*

She tore a world map off the wall. It was one of those detailed kinds where the capitals are pointed out and mountain ranges are sketched in. She tore it over and over and over.

"You don't teach us how to deal with anything, but at least we know when the Declaration of Independence got signed," she shouted. "1776!"

Gris. *Gray. The color of the floor she fell to, surrounded by the world she'd ripped to pieces.*

I think about the video from Fiesta Day of the couple

fighting in the cafeteria. The girl mouthing "How could you." Everyone talked about that video for days, shared it all over social media. Now they'll do the same to my sister.

A bell rings inside the auditorium. Break will be ending soon. My team will settle in their seats and prepare for the speed round. I'm supposed to be the specialist. But I can't go back in there. I can't look out into the audience and see empty seats where my family should be, now that I know why they're missing. Because even if we all smiled in Buelo's room last week, even if Daniella snuck into Ben's play, she isn't better. Nothing is better on this side of the time line. On this page of the calendar.

I dial Uncle Eric's number. He answers on the second ring.

"Cassi? Did you mean to call Jac?"

"No. Can you come pick me up? I'm at Trinity Prep."

"Where are your parents?"

My throat seals up.

"What, Jac?" Uncle Eric's voice sounds far away, like he's covering the receiver. "Oh no. Really? Okay." His voice comes back in clear. "We'll be right there."

I sneak toward the exit, peeling the name tag off my shirt. It makes a sound like the world map tearing off the wall. I throw it into the trash. The moderator passes by me in the hall.

"Sir, can you please tell Mr. Garrison from Eliza T.

Dakota that Cassi Chord had to leave? Thank you."

I'm out the door before he can answer. I hide in a cluster of trees near the parking lot and wait. At one point, Mr. G pokes his head out the door. He looks left, right, left. Then he disappears.

The video plays in my head again, all the way to the end.

Brown and green and blue. Café, verde, azul. *Colors of the earth and trees and water. All of it falling apart.*

I sit between Jac and Ben in the back of Uncle Eric's truck. Leslie is in the passenger seat. Her auburn hair is pinned up, and a briefcase sits by her feet. She turns her head toward me.

"Can I ask you something, Cassi?"

It occurs to me that I haven't really talked to Leslie since Open Mic night.

"Say no," Jac whispers.

"Sure," I say instead.

"Eric tells me this video is unlike your sister. Have you noticed any changes in her as well?"

I think about closed doors, faded music. Sweatpants and soggy cereal in blue bowls. Unanswered *Jeopardy!* questions.

"She's been sad all year. Ever since my Buelo got sick and she started high school."

Leslie nods. "I'm asking you this because I'm a

therapist. At Coastal Wellness. By the mall?"

"I've seen that place," Ben says. I have too. The sign is hard to miss. It's bright white with the name written in blue cursive and three waves curling underneath.

"We help people going through things, similar to Daniella."

"How?" It's not Ben or I who asks. It's Jac. She leans forward in her seat. Leslie's eyebrows lift a little.

"By talking," Leslie replies.

"I've tried to talk to her every day. She won't talk back," Jac says.

"It can be hard to admit that there's something wrong. And I know that what she's going through is hard for you, too. Depression can make it seem like you've lost someone. But she's still in there." Leslie smiles. "I promise. We'll figure this out."

I say the word "depression" under my breath like I'm whispering the answer to a math problem. Jac and Ben look like they're in the middle of a serious scene in one of Ben's plays. Leslie holds out her hand to us. She's always been there—for Open Mic night, and on New Year's, and at our house playing cards in the kitchen. And she understands what's happening to Daniella. I take her hand, and Ben does too. We look at Jac.

"Together," I say to her. Jac stares at Leslie's reached-out hand, takes a breath, and then links her fingers with ours.

Regionals

"I'm with you too. Just can't take my hands off the wheel," Uncle Eric says from the driver's seat. I watch Jac catch his eye in the rearview mirror. He winks at her.

Leslie turns back around. Jac and Ben and I keep our arms looped together like infinity symbols in the backseat until we pull into my driveway.

46

More Writing on the Wall

Daniella and I are on the love seat in the living room. We sit on separate striped cushions and stare at the ground. Our parents stand in front of us like they do when we're about to get a lecture. I expect Mom's eyes to narrow, but instead they fill with tears. Guilt swallows me whole.

"I'm sorry, Mom," I say. "I shouldn't have left the competition without permission."

Daniella grunts. "Well, I'm not sorry. I meant what I said. It's not my fault someone decided to record it."

"You're not in trouble," Dad says. He rubs his forehead.

"Really?" she asks. Dad nods warily and looks at Mom.

"Daniella, I got a recommendation from Leslie for a therapist at her practice," Mom says. "You have an appointment next week."

Dad rubs his face some more. Daniella straightens up.

"No," she says.

I imagine the wall in her chest. The sharp, shattered pieces.

"It's gone beyond what you can handle on your own.

We know you know that," Dad says. Now that he's stopped rubbing, I can see that his eyes are wet too.

But how could she know, even if there were a chapter on it in *The Chemical Property of Life?*

"Please don't make me go," Daniella begs. "I don't want to talk about it."

Mom kneels in front of Daniella and holds her hands.

"I am going to make you go. Because for too long I pretended that this wasn't happening, and I'm sorry for that. I love you. *Te quiero* so, so, so much."

Daniella covers her face with her hands without letting go of Mom's. I touch Daniella's shoulder. Dad places a hand on her back. It feels like "Daniella is depressed" is written on the living room walls in big letters we can't ignore anymore.

Like our signatures in Jac's room, or Mr. G's digits of pi, or "I was here" on the bus seat.

47

Spruce Landing

Daniella's meltdown video has 93,921 views when I get to school on Monday. The total rises to 186,177 by Math Olympics two days later. I walk into Mr. G's classroom, and the stares I receive are like knives. Everyone's eyes stay on me while I sit down, even Mr. G's. No lesson is written on the whiteboard. The words "Congratulations, Regional Champs" are there instead.

Sage raises her hand.

"Mr. G, I don't think it's fair for Cassi to be here. She ditched us and did not contribute to our win."

"That's not true, Sage. She was part of the first round." His tie is black with a white swirl on it in the shape of a tornado.

"Big deal. She was our speed round *specialist.*"

I should open my mouth. Explain myself. But I never speak up like I should. If I'd tried harder to tell someone about the things in Daniella's diary, maybe the video would never have happened.

"That's enough. We're not in the business of kicking people out of Math Olympics." Mr. G hands us all a sheet of paper. "These are the rules for States. They're different from Regionals. Read up, and then we'll review." He doesn't smile or anything when he gives me the handout. I picture his head sticking out of the doors at Trinity Prep, looking for me.

Aaron slides a note across my desk like he did the first day I met him.

Ignore them.

Like we all ignored how bad things really were with Daniella. I slip the note under the list of rules for States and try to read.

There are three rounds in the state-level competition: the round-robin, the timed questions, and the—

"Stupid. Stupid. It's all stupid."

Daniella's voice fills up the room. Sage has her phone out on her lap. I can see the screen, bright and blue, from here. I can hear the world map tearing. My jaw struggles under the weight of tears.

186,178 views.

"Turn it off. Right now." I've never heard Mr. G's voice sound like that. I crunch the rules for States and Aaron's note into a ball and throw it onto the floor. I won't ignore it. And I won't be going to States.

"You know what? You get what you want, Sage. I quit." My backpack thumps against me as I sprint out of the room, out of the school building, all the way to the benches out front. It's warmer today than when

Aaron told me about Juniper. But I feel just as cold.

I curl up on the bench, try to turn myself into a tiny speck. Tiny specks don't cry. Tiny specks' sisters don't get depressed. Tiny specks don't have to know who they are—they're only specks. A leaf falls from the tree above me and lands on my arm. I squeeze myself tighter. *I'm a speck. I'm a speck.*

"Cassi!" Aaron comes running. "Mr. G told me to get you," he says when he's right in front of me.

"I'm not going back."

He picks the leaf off my arm and sits down.

"We know why you left Regionals. Everything will be fine."

Todo estara bien.

Sometimes words aren't enough.

"Sage still played the video in front of everyone."

"She's just being mean. She got to do the speed round, so I don't get why she's even mad." Aaron spins the leaf in his fingers by the stem, and then looks at me.

"She's mad because I held your hand at the Ice Plex," I say.

He reaches for my hand like he did during the friendship skate. He twines our fingers together, squeezes, and lets go.

Maybe I'm a speck, but I'm a speck whose heart is swelling.

"How can I help?" he asks.

I think back to the start of our friendship. Our deal. It doesn't feel like a deal anymore. I don't need a set of Aaron Facts to feel like I know him. He's woven into me the way Jac and Ben are.

"You could tell me the last tree town story," I say.

Aaron drops the leaf.

"Spruce Landing. I guess I've been putting that one off."

My brain tunes in like it does when he starts a story. Everything else falls away.

"What happened?"

"I learned what the memoir was really about," he says.

The leaf is between our shoes. One side is yellow and the other is green. The breeze goes quiet like it's listening.

"Dad always said the memoir was about expanding the borders of our comfort zone. But I was starting to think that if I expanded any further, I'd crack. So I told him that one night." Aaron reaches into his pocket. "And then he showed me this."

He pulls out his phone and scrolls for a minute. When he holds up his screen, I see a picture of a handwritten note. Lines cover the page like it's been folded over and over. I take the phone and start to read.

My loves,

This is the hardest thing I'll ever have to do, but the adventure of our lives together ends here. I am not good for you or for the world we've built. I don't fit in a house or a family portrait. If you ever feel like you might want to come after me, please know that I don't want to be found. I need to be out there, in tree towns, growing. You'll be okay.

Forever,
Tracy

I remember the day of *Bye Bye Birdie* when Mr. Kale approached that woman in the gray sweater like he knew her. Like he'd *found* her.

"He was looking for your mom."

Aaron nods.

"Dad was a lawyer. I should've known something was wrong when he decided to leave it all and start writing a book. When suddenly all he cared about was adventure. But it's not like I had a choice other than to go along. Mom was gone."

I think about Aaron building birdhouses to get his mom to stay, and then leaving them behind like an abandoned neighborhood. Maybe they're still there, withered and mossy but holding on.

"What did you do after he told you?" I ask.

"I got mad. But he begged me to give it one more shot. One last tree town. And we came here." Aaron's face turns red like it does before he speaks a big truth. "But I bet that's not even what Mom meant by 'tree towns.' I don't want to spend my whole life searching for someone who isn't here anymore."

This story doesn't feel careful and plotted the way his stories usually do. It's Aaron spilling out like candy from a piñata.

"Do you think he'll let you stay?" I ask.

"I don't know."

"Do you want to stay?"

He looks at me. "Yeah. A lot. I've never had friends like you, Jac, and Ben before."

The wind blows, and the leaves rustle above our heads. A family of birds sings from somewhere in the branches. I think about the place mats on our kitchen table.

"I've been looking for someone too," I say.

His face creases with concern. "Who?" he asks.

I take a breath and tell him everything. About the things Daniella said at Kindly Vines, about the Welcome to Middle School dance, about the kite at the citadel and Briana from the mall and Buelo's wallet lifted to the cafeteria lights. I tell him about the button on the red shirt. I even tell him about the boy in the Rudolph sweater.

And by the time I finish talking, I realize that the Cassi I thought I was supposed to be, the Cassi from before all those things happened and multiplied, isn't here anymore. I'm like a snake that's shed its skin to make more room to grow. And maybe that's not such a bad thing.

April 20

I snapped. The weight above my head crashed
down harder than it ever has, and I snapped.
The thing is, I do care when the Declaration of
Independence was signed. I care about history
and revolutions. But the weight convinced
me that I don't. The fallen wall in my chest
convinced me that none of it matters at all.

Psycho.

#crazypants.

Why's her hair look like that?

At least she got the question right, people.

What did that map do to her?

I've read all the comments. I've let my fingers
rest on the keyboard, ready to compose an
explanation. I've let myself believe that those
people are right. That I really am a psycho. That
I have done the most embarrassing thing anyone
has ever done. That I should find a rock to hide
under forever.

I had my first therapy session today. My

therapist, Alice, has a kind voice and a small tattoo of an airplane on her wrist. She asks me about my interests, and my goals, and my fears. She uses the word "depression."

It didn't seem to bother her that I kept my arms tight across my chest and wouldn't answer her questions with more than a few words. She acted like we were having a perfectly pleasant conversation.

Maybe I didn't say much. But I did listen.

I've spent a lot of time thinking that there's something wrong with me. That I was an unlikable, broken thing that was making everyone else miserable too.

Alice says that's not true. Yes, something was wrong. The stress in my life turned to deep, heavy sadness in my brain. I needed help.

But there is <u>nothing</u> wrong with <u>me</u>.

I am not broken.

48

Fifty Years

I borrow Daniella's blue romper for the awards ceremony. It's a little too big, but I like the color and how it smells like her. The ceremony is at a banquet hall downtown, the same place where we had Buelo and Buela's fiftieth wedding anniversary party. I wonder if Daniella thinks about that when we walk under the awning at the entrance. I wonder if she remembers standing on the big deck with me, looking out at the water and trying to picture the next fifty years. When my hair tie snapped while we were dancing, she gave me hers. Curls tumbled down to her shoulder blades.

Daniella's been seeing Alice twice a week. She comes home from her sessions looking different. Not happy exactly. But less glassy-eyed and angry. I haven't read her diary since her first visit, so I'm not sure if she's started uncrossing her arms and talking. But I hope so.

Dad holds the door open for us.

"I'm proud of you," he says when Daniella and I walk by. I think he's saying it to both of us. I smile and try to feel proud too.

We make it to the main room. The big hardwood dance floor is surrounded by that generic patterned carpet that all banquet halls seem to have. Round tables are draped in yellow fabric. A chandelier glitters in the center of it all.

"Look, there's Maria." Buela hurries over to a table near the edge to side-kiss an older woman with orange hair. A boy my age sits next to her. I end up beside him when we take the empty seats. The tables are set the proper way, with salad forks and soup spoons and everything. A centerpiece stands in the middle—a tall vase with daffodils stuffed into sand.

"*Tus nietas?*" Maria asks.

"*Sí*, my granddaughters, Cassi and Daniella."

"Nice to meet you." She puts a hand on the boy's shoulder. "This is Javier. It's his second year being awarded." He wears a mustard-colored polo, and his dark hair is slicked back.

"What subject?" I ask him.

"History. You?" My heart smiles a little. He knew the award was going to me. He didn't assume we were here for Daniella, because she looks more like she belongs in the Hispanic Society of Mapleton County. *You belong too.*

"Math."

Waiters start bringing out dinner. The first course is a salad with bleu cheese and walnuts. I eat it all. Daniella pushes the cranberries to the side.

Fifty Years

"Want them?" she asks.

I nod and spear the cranberries right off her plate. It feels so normal, it almost hurts.

A man in a gray suit walks out to the podium during dinner.

"Good evening, everyone. I am Frank Mercado, president of the Hispanic Society. We will now be calling our honorees to the front."

I drop my fork into my lemon chicken. It crashes against the plate and makes everyone at the table look at me. I smile until my parents turn away.

Javier nudges me with his elbow.

"Don't be nervous," he says.

"I didn't know I would have to go up there."

Frank Mercado is still talking. I can't focus on what he's saying.

"It's real easy. You just have to stand and have a picture taken."

I nod. If Jac were here, she'd do something to make me laugh. Aaron would tell a story to distract me. Ben would sing a song about the lemon chicken. But Javier's reassurance works too. Maybe there are friends to be made all over the place.

"Thanks."

Frank Mercado starts to call up the award winners one at a time.

"First is Sierra Ramos. She is a seventh grader at

Trinity Prep. She has been on the honor roll since her first semester of sixth grade, and she is being awarded for her performance in art. She enjoys painting in her spare time. Congratulations, Sierra."

Sierra looks like a twelve-year-old version of my sister, with big curls and bright clothes. She stands next to the podium and rocks back and forth.

More names are called that sound like Sierra's. The award winners line up in a row. I try not to notice how different their names and faces are from mine. *It doesn't matter. It doesn't matter.* He calls another name. *Please don't let it matter.*

"Next is Cassi Chord. She is a seventh grader at Eliza T. Dakota Middle School. She is part of the Math Olympics team and has a perfect A+ average in Math. She enjoys outings with her family in her free time, particularly her sister, who she says is her hero. Congratulations, Cassi."

I look at Daniella. She smiles and imitates taking a deep breath. Her eyes look a little wet.

The carpet seems to stretch on for miles. Applause rings in my ears. Out of the corner of my eye, I see Emilio from Math Olympics. Mr. G must have nominated him, too. He waves at me like I didn't abandon him and the rest of my team at Regionals. I take my spot in the line.

We're at the edge of the dance floor, where my

grandparents slow danced for their fiftieth anniversary.

"Felicidades," the girl next to me whispers, like there isn't anything strange about someone pale and copper-haired being honored by the Hispanic Society of Mapleton County.

"Tu tambien," I answer. *You too.*

Javier gets announced next. He mouths *Good job* at me when he passes by to get to the end of the line. I clap loud when Emilio gets called. After the announcements, a photographer has us move closer together so she can take a picture. I smile until my cheeks are sore while the camera flashes and flashes.

Music starts playing in the middle of dessert, a song made for dancing. The deep bass vibrates in my body. The dance floor fills with people. Parents and grandparents face each other and move, hands linked and arms around each other's waists. You'd think their dances were professionally choreographed, but I think it's their hearts that tell them what to do. The dances are part of them.

I reach for Daniella's hand.

"Let's go out there," I say.

"You want to dance?" She takes another bite of chocolate mousse cake. There's a cherry sauce stain on her plate that looks like the chili on a Pepper's pizza.

"Yes, so much. The music speaks to me."

Javier laughs. He's eaten two pieces of cake.

"Since when?" Daniella asks. Her eyes look like she wants to smile but her mouth hasn't gotten the message yet.

"Since now."

I tug on her arm. I'm not strong enough to lift her like she did to me. But I'm willing to try. She takes the white cloth napkin off her lap and drops it onto the table, then lets me drag her to the dance floor.

"You too, Javier," I call over my shoulder. Javier pushes his chair back so hard, it almost falls, and then follows us.

We claim a spot near the center. Daniella doesn't dance right away. I wish I had her moves to follow but I start doing my own anyway. I sway my hips and feet, swivel my head back and forth. Javier jumps in place with his arms in the air. Daniella shakes her shoulders and claps. I watch her close her eyes a few times, immersed in the music.

Soon Emilio joins our circle. And Sierra from Trinity, who likes painting. And the other award winners too. The songs change, the way everything eventually changes, I guess. But we all keep dancing.

Mr. G was right. It's not a certificate that makes me Spanish, or how I look. It's about the way my heart feels. Like it did at the citadel in San Juan.

Like I fit.

49

Unfair

I'm in my pajamas after the ceremony when there's a knock on my door.

"Come in," I say. The blanket with the faceless princesses is folded at the foot of my bed. It's too warm for fleece now.

Daniella opens the door.

"Can I grab my romper?" she asks. She's wearing pajamas too.

"Yeah." I point to my laundry basket in the corner. The romper lies on top. Daniella walks over and grabs it. When she turns back around, her face has that tired, heartbroken look that's been there all year.

"Why are you sad?" I ask.

She looks up. Her eyes are watery, her shoulders sunken in.

"What?" she asks, like just that one word took all her strength.

"I thought you were feeling better. You were fine at the awards ceremony, and now you look like you did before you went to see Alice." The bottom of my throat prickles, but I refuse to cry.

"It was hard for me just to be there tonight, Cassi. You pulled me onto a dance floor when all I wanted to do was sleep. But I did it. For you."

Everything I've held on to this year floods out of my chest at once, as if I've had a wall in there too and now it's toppling.

"For me? You haven't done anything for me! Not all year. Except close your door, and tell me I wasn't Puerto Rican enough, and ruin every single thing I did to try to help you."

Daniella's eyes are cold, her mouth a straight line. She tucks the romper under her arm. "I knew it would make you feel bad if I said that."

Her words are honest in the way that hurts. The way words hurt when you know you won't forget them for a long, long time. Like "scarecrow." Like "Caucasian (Not Hispanic or Latino)." Like "You're always like *that*."

But why would my sister want to hurt me?

"Why would you say that if you knew?"

Daniella takes a step closer to my bed. I stretch myself across my pillows so that she can't sit down with me.

"I wanted someone else to feel as awful as I did," she says.

"But . . . that's not fair!" I try to visualize my words like numbers in a math equation. They're not adding up.

Sisters don't do that to one another. Especially not sisters who listen to music together and talk with mouths full of toothpaste. "That's mean to make me feel that way. It's not fair that I've had to go through everything this year without you. Buelo, Math Olympics, Aaron. I needed you, Daniella."

I think about all the seasons that have passed. The burnt-orange leaves, steep hills covered in snow, the trees starting to sprout pink flowers. She hasn't been there for any of it.

I'm so mad, my body can't hold it all in. I leap off my bed and tug the drawer of the nightstand open, take the stack of calendar pages out. I turn around to face Daniella and throw them at her. I throw every single day she's missed back into her face. I want them to bury her the way they've buried me. The pages flurry to the ground. Daniella stands there, like a statue, her hands curled into fists.

"I knew it. I knew you were going into my room. I just hoped you weren't *that* sneaky!" she shouts.

"Well, I was. I've been going into your room and reading your diary since September. I was *trying* to figure out a way to make you feel better!" I admit. I watch the truth sink in. Daniella's eyes are narrow and fiery.

We've reached our highest pressure.

She kicks at the calendar pages. October twenty-seventh flies into the air, telling me *Be kind whenever possible. It is always possible.* February third hits my ankle.

Don't forget that some things count more than other things.

"I can't just snap my fingers and be fine, Cassi. I can't talk to you about Buelo, when just thinking about it feels like being hit by a wrecking ball. You say it's not fair that I haven't been around, but guess what else isn't fair? Expecting me to be. Using my private thoughts to *manipulate* me."

The anger in me withers. I was so sure that I was doing the right thing. But was it never up to me to make Daniella better with fires or rice or music?

I want to get to the part where we end up like diamonds.

"I just miss you so much," I say. My voice cracks. Tears spring to my eyes. "I want you to be my best friend again." The hurt I've been feeling all year streaks down my face.

Daniella walks to my bed. The calendar pages slide under her feet. She sits on the edge and taps my polka-dotted comforter. I take the spot next to her, leaving space between us.

"I'm still your best friend. And you're still mine. But I can't be your hero right now. It's too much responsibility."

"I never meant to put responsibility on you." The words rush out of me.

"I know you didn't mean to. And I want to be here for you still, as best I can. I want to be out on that dance floor. But for now maybe we can take it one song at a time."

If I really want Daniella to feel better, then I have to let her do it in her own way. Just like I'm figuring out how to be me through all these changes.

"I'm okay with that."

Daniella sets up my speaker, then leans into my pillows. Our favorite breakup song plays, and even though it's sad, it's ours.

"When's the last time you read my diary?" she asks in the middle of the chorus.

"I stopped after the first time you saw Alice."

She walks out of my room, over the calendar pages, past the pebble CASSANDRA and the seashell DANIELLA. Her door stays cracked open when she comes back. She sits down on my bed again, her diary in her lap.

"I'm supposed to start trying to be more open. I used to think I'd be bothering people if I talked about my feelings. Alice says that's not true." Daniella opens to a page near the back. She looks up at me. "I'm sealing this with a padlock."

I nod, thinking about something I didn't before. Maybe the wall in Daniella's chest didn't fall to let the sadness escape. Maybe it fell so that other people could get in.

Daniella takes a breath like she's letting something go, and starts to read.

May 1

Alice wanted me to close my eyes and picture a happy place. I didn't at first, because that's what everyone says to do. If it were that easy, wouldn't we all be closing our eyes and going somewhere else all the time?

"Trust me," she said. She says that a lot. I'm starting to.

So I closed my eyes. I tried not to think about much at all. I let my heart decide what happy place to take me to.

I ended up at the biggest bioluminescent bay in Puerto Rico. Buelo and Buela brought us there on our last trip. We took a boat out onto the water at night. I stood at the edge of the boat with Cassi. Waves lapped up against the side. The breeze was cool and smelled like salt.

"I see it," Cassi said, and pointed.

The water stretched out for miles. Hundreds of speckled organisms glimmered under the surface, like stars.

May 1

I remember thinking that the sky and the sea looked the same.

I remember thinking that even in the deepest, darkest blackness, there's light.

50

Lesson Thirty-Two

I take deep breaths outside Mr. G's classroom on Wednesday. Aaron fans my face with his hand.

"Are you sure about this? There's a reason we're mathletes and not writers," he says.

"Says the expert storyteller."

I push the hair away from my face. The school still hasn't turned the air-conditioning on, so I'm sweating through my shirt. I wish we were in Juniper's zero-degree weather, or the snowy garden in North Sapling.

Sometimes when I'm around Aaron, I have to stop my brain from counting down the seconds. It's hard not knowing if one day we'll run out of time, and then he'll be off to another tree town, even though his Dad promised this would be the last one.

"If your dad tries to get you to leave, we'll do a skit," Ben said two weeks ago, when they first opened the pool at Lakeside Townhouses. *"About how we'll all fall apart if you leave us."*

"Or maybe we'll just hide you," Jac offered. We stared at her.

"Where are you going to put me?" Aaron asked.

Lesson Thirty-Two

Jac smiled. The turquoise pool water turned chilly. "You'll see."

Sage and Allie walk past us and through Mr. G's door. Sage's eyes are still arrows, but Allie kind of smiles. Mr. G is finishing writing his lesson on the board. *Lesson Thirty-Two of Mathematics: If all else fails, start over.*

"Okay. I'm ready," I say.

We walk in. Aaron goes to his desk, and I head for the front of the class. Mr. G looks surprised but makes it all exaggerated, with his hands over his mouth and his eyebrows lifted.

"Cassi, you came back."

"I want to say something to the club," I explain, before I can talk myself out of it.

"Please, go ahead." He bows and puts his arm out like he's giving me the floor. Everyone's eyes lift up to meet mine.

There are notebooks on everyone's desks, a lesson on the whiteboard about starting over. I breathe deep and try to be brave, like Ben at the Open Mic and Aaron when he told me about Spruce Landing.

"I'm not good at telling stories, but I am good with numbers. The video of my sister has been viewed roughly three hundred thousand times. I estimate that if each person watches it about three times, then one hundred thousand people have seen my sister hit rock bottom.

Out of those people, zero of them will understand why she did what she did. Because you can't know everything about a person by looking at them. If you had to list things about me just by the way I look, you probably wouldn't say that I love math. Or that I have a Buelo with dementia and a Buela who calls me "*Fantasma.*" And I can guess with ninety-four percent certainty that you would not say I'm Puerto Rican. But I am. All those things are true. I have two halves of me, and the way they add together makes me who I am. Cassi Chord."

I start to feel the weight of everyone's eyes on me. Aaron nods at me to keep going. Sage's stare isn't so sharp.

The door rattles. I look over and see Jac and Ben watching through the narrow window built into the wood. They drop to the ground. I swallow a laugh and keep going.

"I'm sorry for abandoning you all. I was the speed specialist, and I should have been there. You've calculated by now that I saw the video for the first time at Regionals. That's why I left. This group has become another important part of me, and I don't want to lose it. So I hope you can all forgive me, because in case you can't tell, I really, really want to go to States."

Mr. G has a fake license plate from Hawaii in the back of his room, with the word "Aloha" written on it. I remember learning once that "Aloha" can be used for either "hello" or "good-bye." I wait in front of *Lesson Thirty-Two* for my teammates to decide what it means.

Summer, Again

51

Founders' Day Fireworks

Jac, Ben, and I lie on the hill outside Lakeside Townhouses for the Founders' Day fireworks. Jac's camouflage comforter is soft, and the weather is my favorite kind, where I'm comfortable in a hoodie and shorts. There were times this year when I didn't think we'd find our way back here, to the million stars of a Mapleton summer night.

The sound of laughter drifts up from the bottom of the hill. Daniella tosses a football to Jenna. Two boys stand in between them and try to break up her pass. I know she won't sit with us this year, because things aren't exactly the same as they used to be.

Someone else is missing too.

"They're going to start soon," Ben says. He was in the Mapleton Community Theater production of *Cats* this afternoon. There are thick black whiskers still painted on his face.

"I think they're going to start right *meow*," Jac says, and grins. She's added raised eyebrows to her signature smile. I haven't told her, but it's more goofy than scary now.

"You're better than that." I give her joke a thumbs-down. I think Aaron would too if he were here.

From our spot on the hill, I can see the stretch of water where they'll set off the fireworks, dark except for splashes of moonlight. I can hear my sister's laughter.

Someone sits next to me.

"You're late," I say.

"Sorry. Dad and I were recording a radio interview," Aaron says.

"Our little celebrity."

Mr. Kale found a publisher for his memoir. It's called *Out There, In Tree Towns, Growing*. It didn't end up being what he'd planned. It's about a father and son who searched for someone in five tree towns and found home instead.

"I was supposed to be the famous one in this group. Look at my commitment," Ben says, and points to his pink painted nose.

"If I have to wear that, then I don't want to be famous," Aaron replies. The sides of our hands touch on the camouflage comforter. I smile into the dark, my heart buzzing.

Aaron has his state championship pin fastened to his hoodie. I keep mine in my bedroom on the table I made in Metals, next to the newest figurine from Titi Celina. An elephant, for Buelo. Because elephants never forget.

The first firework goes off. It's blue, and so big that

it takes up the whole sky. A few more follow, green and yellow and purple. They shine and then fade into smoke that looks like ghosts. I'm not so afraid of *fantasmas* anymore. The fireworks are turning into crooked hearts when Daniella steps into my view.

"Hey," she says. She sits down in front of me and leans back, her head landing in my lap.

"What are you doing?" I ask.

"It's tradition." She says it like it's the most obvious thing.

There might always be pieces of my sister that are sadder than the rest, like deep blue shards in a stained-glass window. This past year will be a part of us. A part of our story. But it's not the whole story. We have lots of chapters left to go. And one day, maybe fifty years from now, we'll be able to look back and see how this year fit into the equation of our lives.

I gather a section of her hair and tie it into a braid. When I get to the bottom, I untie it, and begin again.

Acknowledgments

Cassi and Aaron have had a place in my head since 2014. Their story has changed a lot since then. Would you believe it if I told you that this book used to take place at camp? Or that Aaron held a huge grudge against Cassi? Or that Jac's hair changed color through magic? I have many people to thank for helping me take my (bad) ideas and turn them into the story about friendship and family and belonging that I always wanted to write.

Thank you to Krista Vitola, my amazing editor, who guided me to the true heart of this book and stuck with me while I worked to dig it out. I am so thankful for your encouragement and vision. Thank you to Catherine Laudone and the rest of the team at Simon & Schuster Books for Young Readers. Thank you to Bara MacNeill, Jenica Nasworthy, and Morgan York for your careful copyedits. Thank you to Krista Vossen and Ira Sluyterman van Langeweyde for designing and illustrating a cover that made me cry the first time I saw it and several times after that.

I am endlessly grateful to my agent, Zoe Sandler, for your guidance, positivity, and support.

Thank you to my sensitivity readers, Melissa J., Christina K., and Camellia M., for your openness, and for working with me on Daniella's experiences. Your empathy and honesty shone through in your feedback.

My family stands by me through everything, and the process of writing this book was no exception. Dad, Mom, and Crissy—we are a team. I've been blessed with a big group of cousins, aunts, uncles, and grandparents who all made me want to write a book about family.

I could never say thank you enough to my friends. There have been brunches attended, trips taken, new seasons of shows watched, pizza eaten, big life steps made, and small, perfect moments spent together. I will resist the urge to list your initials like an AIM profile from 2005, but you know who you are.

Thank you, God, for making it my dream to write books.

And thank you, reader, for visiting this tree town. I hope you enjoy your stay.

Author's Note

My papa, Tito Velez-Rivera, taught me Spanish in a song. Through him, I learned how to say "pencil" and "teacher" and "door." I learned *te quiero mucho*. And he continued to say *te quiero mucho*, even as his memory failed.

Being Puerto Rican has been as much a part of me as being a writer. I wouldn't be who I am without the Spanish-language masses I went to on Sundays, or my nana's rice and beans. But in some ways, it has felt like an invisible part of me. It has left me wondering how one minute I could be in a kitchen with my family, who speak in voices that sound like yelling if you aren't used to it, a pot on each burner and pernil in the oven, and the next, I'm somewhere no one would guess where my family came from. It has led to surprised looks, awkward moments, and unsteady check marks in boxes. But more important, it has led to so, so much love.

I had to learn to feel like I belonged when I was sure that I didn't. I had to learn that it was more important to be out in the sunshine than to turn tan from it. And this doesn't just apply to heritage. There are so many things to feel not *enough* of. Cool enough, smart enough, popular enough. I wrote Cassi's story because in the end, it was the strength inside her and the people around her, both sides of her family and the family of friends she created on her own, that helped her see that she was exactly who she was supposed to be.

And you are exactly who you're supposed to be.

I try to remember that the way I remember my papa's song, teaching me to say "pencil" in Spanish.